BLANCHE
ON THE LAM

Books by Barbara Neely
Blanche on the Lam
Blanche Among the Talented Tenth
Blanche Cleans Up
Blanche Passes Go

BLANCHE ON THE LAM

A BLANCHE WHITE MYSTERY

BARBARA NEELY

The characters and events portrayed in this book are fictitious. Any similarity to real persons, living or dead, is coincidental and not intended by the author.

ISBN: 1941298389
ISBN 13: 9781941298381

Published by Brash Books, LLC
12120 State Line #253,
Leawood, Kansas 66209

www.brash-books.com

For my sister Vanessa

ONE

"Have you anything to say for yourself?" The judge gave Blanche a look that made her raise her handbag to her chest like a shield.

"Your Honor...I'm sorry...I..."

"Sorry? It most certainly is sorry! This is the fourth, I repeat, the fourth time you've been before this court on a bad-check charge. Perhaps some time in a jail cell will convince you to earn your money before you spend it, like the rest of us. Thirty days and restitution!"

"But, Your Honor..." Blanche's legs were suddenly weak. Her hands were freezing. Beads of sweat popped out on her nose. She wanted to tell the judge that a jail cell was cruel and unusual punishment for a person who panicked in slow elevators. She also wanted to ask him where the hell he got off, lying about her like that! This was her second, not her fourth charge. Furthermore, just as she'd done the last time, she would have made good on the checks even if she hadn't been summoned to court. Hadn't she already covered three of the five checks she'd written? And right here in her handbag she had the forty-two-fifty she still owed, plus fifty dollars for the fine—same as the judge had made her pay last time. But last time she'd had a judge with his mind already on the golf course. He'd hardly bothered to look at her. There'd been no talk of jail that time.

"Your Honor," she began again.

The bang of the gavel was like a shot fired in the room. "Next case!"

"Come along." The matron's hand was pale as plaster against the deep blackness of Blanche's upper arm. Blanche looked around the courtroom, but no one was interested enough to look back. She was already being replaced before the judge by a stooped, sad-faced white man with cut-up shoes and hands red as raw meat.

She was taken to an anteroom with metal tables and chairs that looked like every prison movie she'd ever seen. A dark blond, bullet-headed boy in jeans and cowboy boots sat on a long bench against the far wall. Sheriff Stillwell stood beside him, his short, bandy legs bowed beneath the weight of his belly. His right hand was on his pistol, his eyes were boring a hole in the opposite wall. Blanche tried to catch the boy's eye, to see and be seen by someone before they both disappeared into...She clutched her stomach and half-turned to the matron.

"I gotta use the toilet!"

The matron gave her an annoyed frown, looked at her watch, then pulled Blanche through another doorway that led onto the back corridor. Diagonally across the hall, between the staircase and the men's room, was a door marked LADIES.

A dingy skylight threw murky light down onto a cracked marble floor. A mottled basin and a toilet stall were crowded together in a space hardly large enough for the two women. Blanche entered the stall and padded the seat with toilet paper before sitting down to ease her bowels with as little noise as possible.

"I'll be right out in the hall," the matron muttered in a disgusted tone.

Blanche put her elbows on her knees and fumed. Thoughts scurried in and out of her mind like mice in an abandoned kitchen. I shoulda known better, she told herself. She rocked back and forth on the commode. Shoulda known. She wound her arms tightly round her body, comforting herself in the same way she did her children. She closed her eyes and saw the judge accusing her of being lower than snake shit. She opened her eyes, only to see where she was and where she was headed.

She knew she should be making a mental list of all she would need in jail that Durham County would surely not provide. She should be planning what she wanted her mother to tell the children. She should be convincing herself that she could and would survive the next thirty days. Instead, she raged at the judge for being an unfair dickbrain, and at herself for ignoring all the signs of trouble coming:

The way her hand had itched and throbbed at the same time as she'd stood in her kitchen reading the court summons; the way the glass she was drinking from just before she left the house for court had suddenly developed a crack while she held it to her lips. She'd ignored both events despite her claim that reading people and signs, and sizing up situations, were as much a part of her work as scrubbing floors and making beds. She threw her head back to keep the tears from falling and wished the most vain hope of all—the chance to rearrange her life so that she would not be in this situation.

Shoulda stayed in New York, she told herself; at least I made enough to cover my checks. And she could do a lot better there now that dotcom money was adding names to the list of New Yorkers with more money than anyone ought to have. But the day Taifa and Malik came home from school and told her about the man who'd tried to entice them into his van with the promise of a Run-DMC tape was the day Blanche knew they had to leave New York. She'd gathered her children and her belongings and headed for the relative safety of Farleigh, North Carolina, where she and the children had been born.

And this was what it had gotten her.

Why the hell hadn't she borrowed the money and paid it directly to the stores and utilities instead of writing those damned checks? Too proud, she remonstrated with herself. Still dreaming. Still hoping to find an employer willing to pay for a full-service domestic instead of the bunch of so-called genteel Southern white women for whom she currently did day work. Most of them seemed to think she ought to be delighted to swab their toilets and trash cans for a pittance. Farleigh was not New York, or even Raleigh or Durham, and certainly not Chapel Hill, where there were plenty of professional and academic folks eager for good help. Farleigh was still a country town, for all its pretensions. The folks who lived here and had money, even the really wealthy ones, thought they were still living in slavery days, when a black woman was grateful for the chance to work indoors. Even at the going rate in Farleigh she'd found no black people in town who could afford her—not that working for black people ensured good treatment, sad to say.

Too proud. That was always her problem. The first time she'd been summoned to court about her checks she hadn't known what to expect and hadn't asked anyone. She didn't want to admit that she worked six days a week and still didn't make enough money to take care of herself and her children. Her low salary wasn't her fault, but it still made her feel like a fool, as if she'd fallen for some obvious con game.

"Hurry up in there, gal!"

The matron's gruff voice ripped away all pretext that time was standing still. Blanche cast about for something to hang on to, something that would help her get through what lay ahead. Had she been the woman her mother had raised her to be, she would have prayed. Instead, she decided to get a lawyer. Shoulda had a lawyer all along, she chided herself; not to have done so seemed stupid now. After all, she'd intended no crime. If four of her employers hadn't gone out of town without paying her, she'd have had enough money in the bank to cover the checks. She was smoothing down the skirt of her dress and still fighting off the desire to scream, and plead, and wallow in her fear, when an explosion of voices erupted in the hall.

The sounds of men shouting questions and the shuffling of feet came clearly over the transom. Blanche picked up her handbag and left the stall without flushing the commode. She stood listening as the noise in the corridor grew even louder. She eased the outer door open just a crack.

The matron was standing to the left of the door, almost in front of the men's room. She was facing down the hall, away from Blanche, toward a group of men with cameras, note pads, and microphones. They were circling someone Blanche couldn't see but who she was sure must be the county commissioner recently charged with accepting bribes.

She was positive he wouldn't get thirty days. A little bad publicity, and a lot of sympathy from people who might easily be in his position, was about all he'd get. She turned her head and looked at the stairs on the other side of the bathroom—stairs that led down to the outside, according to the EXIT sign above the stairwell.

Blanche opened the bathroom door just wide enough for her to slip into the hall. She crab-walked to the waiting stairs. The part of her that had been raised to believe in and obey the law was urging her to turn back before it was too late. But turning back was made impossible by the thought of thirty days of walls pressing closer, of living behind a door she couldn't open. She egged herself on with the thought of the commissioner getting off scot-free.

She ran down the stairs on tiptoe. She flattened as much of herself against the clammy green wall as she could, for a stout woman, and wished she could fade into it. One flight. Two flights. She could still hear reporters upstairs screaming questions in high-pitched voices. She concentrated on the door marked EXIT, ordering it to be unlocked, to not be surrounded by sheriff's deputies on the other side.

A great sob welled up in her chest at the sight of the dark underground parking lot she found when she pulled open the heavy door. She didn't see anyone, but she knew better than to run. A running black person was still a target of suspicion in this town, even if the runner was a woman. She crouched quite low and, despite her forty years, zigzagged across the parking lot toward the opening, bright with outside light.

She was in back of the courthouse. She stepped out onto the pavement, straightened her dress, and walked quickly away from the courthouse and the few blocks of downtown stores. She moved with as much of an air of a woman going about serious business as she could muster—eyes straight ahead and a serious set to her mouth. Her ears strained for a siren or the sound of her name being called in a way that meant "Halt!" She fought the urge to look behind her or to look for streets that might take her to her neighborhood. Anybody who watched TV knew it was dumb to try to hide out at home. A young white woman with a small child gave her a curious look. Blanche hurried around the next corner. She knew she'd be less noticeable if she slowed down, but her legs wouldn't let her. Her brain had given them the "Run!" message and they were bent on following that order.

She had a naturally long stride and generally walked so fast that her friend Ardell refused to walk anywhere with her. Now she whipped around corners and down unfamiliar streets until her heart pounded on the wall of her chest like a prisoner demanding release. The pavement rushed up to slap the bottoms of her feet—hard, jarring slaps made more lethal by her size. Though she didn't consider herself fat, she did admit to having big bones and hips. And breasts and forearms to match, when it came right down to it. Only her legs were on the smallish side. However, they didn't have any trouble carrying her as fast and as far as she wanted to go.

For the first time in her life, she wished for the kind of gray and rainy day when people seemed to pull inside themselves, unwilling to look out and see the world, see other people. See her. She walked on at top speed until she was so out of breath she was forced to stop. She leaned against a nearby tree. She needed to think, make a plan.

Around her lay the clipped and tamed lawns of one of the sidewalkless worlds where she went to scrub floors and make beds for women whose major life goals included attempting to supervise her doing their housework, and bragging to their friends about how well they'd trained her. This particular neighborhood was at the high end of the ones in which she currently worked. No buildings could be seen from the road, but the presence of solid old houses with more than one kind of domestic help could be felt in the air. She wished she had a little white child to push in a carriage or a poodle on a leash so she'd look as though she belonged there.

She walked along the narrowing road until she reached a street sign—Grace Road and Cranberry Way. Where had she seen Cranberry Way before? She took a few more steps before her memory caught up with her. She stopped to root around in her sturdy, all-purpose black handbag. She pulled out a small, dog-eared notebook, wet the tip of her finger, and quickly flipped through it until she found the page with the note she'd made. She'd scribbled the name of the family so that now she couldn't make it out, except that it began with a *C* and ended with an *S*. The address was clear—One Cranberry Way, 8:30. The weeklong job she'd canceled out of this morning was around here somewhere.

It was a Ty-Dee Girls job. She didn't like working for domestic agencies, particularly this one. The wages were even lower than what she got on her own, and the people who ran it were nasty as castor oil. But they were a steady source of extra income while she was building up her private clientele. She'd known for weeks that she wasn't going to take the Ty-Dee job. She'd lined up more lucrative work for the week. She'd meant to call the agency days ago, but it had slipped her mind, until this morning. They'd been pissed as hell that she'd canceled at the last minute. They weren't so likely to find a replacement for her with no notice. If she got lucky, this could be the perfect place to hide until she could get safely out of town. If Ty-Dee had already sent someone to the job, Blanche would claim her showing up was some sort of mix-up and just tiptoe away. Now to find the place.

She hurried down Cranberry Way, hoping she was going in the right direction. A sharp curve in the road turned out to be its end. She was smack up against a high wrought-iron fence with arrowhead spikes along the top.

Blanche turned and stared down the road she'd just traveled. The enormity of what she'd done settled over her like one of those gray clouds she'd been wishing for earlier. Instead of looking for a hiding place, she wished she could just get out of town. Find the nearest highway and get as far away from Farleigh as she could get, that's what she wanted to do. But she had more than her wants to consider; there was also Mama and the kids.

Lord! She could see and hear the whole thing—the sheriff banging on Mama's door, Mama huffing and fussing while the sheriff was questioning her about Blanche's whereabouts, opening her closet doors, leaving footprints on her linoleum. Mama would definitely throw a conniption! Would she be able to keep the kids from knowing what was going on? Blanche shook her head to dislodge the picture of a beefy deputy dragging Taifa and Malik away from Mama's outstretched arms. She told herself that her being a fugitive wasn't reason enough for the county to take over the care of a couple of black kids with a grandmother more than willing to keep them. She knew she was just frightening herself, as if her situation weren't scary enough. Still, the picture of her sobbing children wouldn't go away.

She'd been reluctant to take on the role of parent to her dead sister's two children, even though she'd promised her sister she would do so. It had taken a year as an adult runaway in California before she could finally face the task. When she'd returned from

California—from what her friend Ardell called "Blanche's first chance"—she'd taken responsibility for the children even though her mother, who'd had them while Blanche was away, was not at all happy about giving them up.

"First you run off hollerin' about how you don't want these children takin' over your life. Now you come back here and break my heart by draggin' my grandbabies off to New York! Don't no child need to be in New York!" her mother had told Blanche when she came for the children. It was her next words on the subject that now bothered Blanche: "Better not be no next time. I might not let 'em go." Her mother's voice was so clear in Blanche's head they might have been standing face to face. The "next time" her mother had warned her against was equally present. Blanche rubbed her upper arms and shivered. Somewhere nearby a mourning dove seconded her growing despair.

TWO

"There you are!"

Blanche whirled around. The left half of a woman's face with one large, gray-blue eye was peering out at her from an opening in the fence.

"At least you could have phoned to say you'd be late! I've been trying to get your agency on the phone for hours. But I knew that if you came at all, you'd come to this gate! I just knew it!" Triumph struggled with peevishness for control of the woman's voice.

"That agency always sends you people to this gate, even though I've told them repeatedly not to do so." She raised her arms above her head and tugged at the high gate. The bottom of her apple-green blouse crept out of the waistband of her skirt. A bit of beige silk slip hung from beneath the hem.

"Well, don't just stand there! We want to leave immediately after lunch." The woman stood back from the gate and motioned Blanche inside.

"Where's your bag?" The woman's pale eyes made contact with Blanche's dark ones for half a second. The woman's face was older than her light, breathy voice. Not-so-small wrinkles branched out from her eyes and down her cheeks. Wavy lines creased her forehead, and the skin around her mouth was beginning to pucker. Her sharp-featured face with its wide-set eyes and high, sloping forehead reminded Blanche of the pet ferret her Uncle Willie used to keep for hunting rabbits. Cropped blond hair accentuated the point of her chin and her rather long neck.

She was a few inches shorter than Blanche's five foot seven and looked anywhere from thirty-five to fifty. Whatever her age, she was in better shape than Blanche, flat-bellied and wiry. She held herself very straight but relaxed, in the way of women who have been schooled in posture.

"Never mind," she added, saving Blanche from having to think up an excuse for not having a suitcase. "You can take care of that tomorrow. You're about Bernice's size. She always leaves a spare uniform at the country house. You'll just have to wear your street clothes until we get there." She gave Blanche a somewhat pained look before continuing along the cobblestone path.

Blanche was reminded of old lady Ivy, out on Long Island. She couldn't stand to see the help in regular clothes, either. Might mistake them for human beings. Blanche chopped down her usually wide stride to match the pace of the woman in front of her. A stone could walk faster, Blanche tsked to herself.

"Cook left a cold lunch." The woman turned her head toward Blanche. "You need only set up a buffet in the dining room. We'll serve ourselves. We'll lunch early. I want to leave for the country as soon as possible." She took a deep breath. "Of course, there's the washing up to be done.

"Darn it!" The woman lurched forward as though she'd tripped over some unseen obstacle. She recovered herself and continued walking and talking as though nothing had happened.

Blanche thought of her Aunt Sarah. Blanche had actually seen Aunt Sarah continue to expound on the best way to smoke a turkey while sitting in a sea of oranges she'd knocked from a bin at the supermarket after stumbling over nothing anyone could see. Aunt Sarah had continued her turkey-smoking instructions even while Blanche and one of the bag boys were hoisting her to her feet.

"There is no other help in the house, just now." The woman raised her pink-nailed hand as if to ward off some protest or question from Blanche.

"Of course, you'll be getting the meals and seeing to the house in the country," the woman told her.

Blanche wondered if rich girls took classes in how to impose on the help by making an impossible workload sound like a breeze.

"It is aired and ready for us, however. And we're very informal there. No large dinner parties, few guests. Although we always maintain a high standard."

A wry smile lifted the corners of Blanche's mouth. Life did seem to be poking fun at her, sometimes. Even on the run she had to clean up after people.

"We always give our regular staff vacation when we go to the country. That's why you're here." The woman turned her head and gave Blanche a smile with more width than warmth in it. And because you're trying to make it on the cheap with just one staff person, Blanche added to herself. What was it about money that made people who had it not want to spend it? Blanche gave the woman her own shark's tooth smile, along with a demure "Yes, ma'am." She was relieved to hear the regular help was away. She wondered if the woman was as direct and fast-talking with other people who were not the help.

The woman stopped and turned so suddenly that Blanche almost bumped into her. She examined Blanche's face. "You *have* worked for us before, haven't you?" A vertical frown creased the middle of her forehead. "I specifically asked the agency to send someone who knew our...routine. My aunt's...I don't seem to remember your face..." Her eyes narrowed slightly.

Blanche forced her mouth into a toothy grin and blinked rapidly at the woman. "Oh, yes, ma'am!" Blanche's voice was two octaves higher than usual. "You remember me! I worked for ya'll about six months ago. I think one of ya'll's regular help was out sick? Or maybe had a death in the family?" She gave the woman an expectant look.

The woman's face remained blank for a moment. "Oh, yes, of course." She quickly turned and continued walking along the path. "My memory is just terrible of late," she told Blanche over her shoulder. "So much to think about, to remember...so much on my..."

Blanche smiled and nodded. She ain't got no more idea what's going on in her house than a jackrabbit. Blanche had guessed as much. The woman hadn't even bothered to ask her name. That was just fine. The last thing Blanche needed right now was a truly interested employer. But she was sorry for the permanent help. This was the kind of employer who responded to your need for a surgeon with a bag of dated, cast-off clothes.

The house they approached was large, many-winged, graceful, and of that peculiar pink brick which Blanche remembered seeing only in this part of the country. Blanche believed in the power of houses. She'd worked inside too many of them to act—as most people did—as though a house were just a building. She could often tell what a house was going to be like by the way it either fit into the landscape or imposed itself upon it.

This house rose from a bed of flowers and shrubs that spoke of a builder and a once-a-week gardener, both with an eye for blending nature and architecture. But this house had nothing to say to her, personally. Much like the woman who lived in it, the house recognized her only as a function. Fortunately, she wasn't going to be there long enough for it to matter.

She followed the woman up three steps to a flagstone patio and through French doors into a room that smelled of leather and was lined with so many books it could have been a nook in the New York Public Library. The woman opened a door on the far side of the room. Blanche followed her down a long hall, around a corner, past four or five other doors, and down a dark, uncarpeted, and narrower corridor into a large, bright kitchen.

It was at least as attractive, well designed, and well appointed as any of the kitchens she'd known in New York. And it was larger than most—a microwave, plus two built-in, eye-level ovens, a rotisserie, a double-door refrigerator and freezer built into the wall, an eight-burner range, copper-bottomed pots hanging from the ceiling, a wealth of kitchen cabinets, and, in the middle of the floor, a butcher-block work station complete with sink and garbage-disposal unit. It was a kitchen so different from the rickety range and dripping tap in the house Blanche lived in that she didn't think they ought to be called by the same name.

"I'm sure you can find everything you need." The woman looked around the kitchen like a bellhop checking the towels. "There will be three at table for lunch. We shall want lunch at eleven-forty-five. You may use the room up these stairs, first door on the left, to freshen up. You won't be coming back here, so don't leave anything behind." The woman gave Blanche an expectant look.

"Yes, ma'am," Blanche told her. "I understand." Blanche thought the woman was about to add something, when the phone rang. The woman turned abruptly and pushed a swinging door that Blanche assumed separated the kitchen from the rest of the house. The phone fell silent in mid-ring.

Blanche leaned against the butcher-block station and let her breath out in a slow, steady stream. If the agency had found a replacement for her, that person had to show up pretty soon. Then what? Miz Mistress was sure to call the sheriff. To save face after having let a stranger into her house, she might even claim that Blanche had pushed her way in uninvited or tried to steal something. If I had any sense, Blanche thought, I'd leave now. But which way was out? A look out the kitchen window showed her a walled-in yard that didn't have a wooded path like the one they'd taken to the house. If she went through the front of the house she might run into the woman, and she certainly couldn't find her way through the house to the way she'd entered.

She heard a noise on the other side of the swinging door and quickly slipped on the bright-eyed but vacant expression behind which she'd hid from the woman so far. Blanche had learned long ago that signs of pleasant stupidity in household help made some employers feel more comfortable, as though their wallets, their car keys, and their ideas about themselves were all safe. Putting on a dumb act was something many black people considered unacceptable, but she sometimes found it a useful place to hide. She also got a lot of secret pleasure from fooling people who assumed they were smarter than she was by virtue of the way she looked and made her living.

"That was your agency," the woman said as she entered the kitchen. "They called to say you weren't going to be able to make it until tomorrow! Can you imagine! I gave them quite a lecture about their lack of efficiency."

The woman looked so pleased with herself, Blanche wondered if she got her jollies from telling people off—or maybe it was the novelty that perked her up.

"They want you to call them. Perhaps after lunch." She turned her head to give Blanche another of those mouth-only smiles and bumped into a chair. "Ow!" The woman pushed the chair away from her as though it had been the attacker. She turned sharply and left the kitchen as though the whole room might be in cahoots with the chair.

That was the second time Blanche had seen her stumble. There was something about the woman's clumsiness that reminded Blanche of Deke Williams, the stunt man for whom she'd once worked. She used to love to listen to Deke explain things like how to take the least painful fall, and how Charlie Chaplin had raised falling to an art form. There was certainly nothing arty about this person's stumbling around.

Blanche looked at her watch—10:45. How could so much have happened to her in so few hours? She opened the refrigerator. Three of its spacious shelves held artfully decorated and arranged platters of cold meats and salads, as well as two trays of yeast rolls waiting for the oven. Good. She had plenty of time to make her phone calls. She'd noticed that the woman had gone to the front of the house to answer the phone instead of using the one hanging on the kitchen wall. She wondered if this was the colored-only phone—this was Dixie, after all. But she thought it more likely that the woman had been expecting a call she didn't want overheard. Blanche went to the swinging door and pushed it gently to see if her employer was anywhere around. Blanche didn't want her phone calls overheard either. Beyond the swinging door was a pantry with shelves and a narrow counter on either side. There was another swinging door at the other end of the pantry. It lead to the dining room. Blanche took a quick peek. No one there. She listened. Nothing. She decided to take the chance while she had it and went back to the kitchen to make her calls.

"It's me, Mama."

"I was wondering where you was. I want you to stop by the…"

"Listen, Mama. I only got a second." Blanche lowered her voice and kept her eyes on the swinging door. The urgency in her tone stopped her mother from objecting to being interrupted in mid-order.

"I wanted to tell you I'm safe. I…"

"What you mean, 'safe'?" her mother wanted to know. "I don't know nothin' about you not being safe!"

"I can't explain right now, Mama. Just trust me and take care of the kids until I can…If the sheriff or anyone asks, say you haven't talked to me. Say you figure I've run off to New Orleans, like I been talking about doing. But please don't let the kids hear you say that…They're all right, ain't they? Yes, I know you're not a lying woman, Mama, so you know it must be important, or I wouldn't ask you to do it. I'll call you again just as soon as I can. Give Taifa and Malik my love, and tell them I'm sorry I couldn't call while they were home, and tell them I'll…"

"Don't you worry about these children," Miz Cora interrupted. "My grandbabies is just fine here with me, just fine."

For a few seconds after her mother hung up, Blanche continued to hold the receiver to her ear and stare at the wall in front of her. Her mother's words hung in her mind like heavy weather. There was no mistaking her tone. Blanche felt herself a soldier being forewarned of the coming war.

It seemed ironic that after California, and all of her resistance and anger over being saddled with Taifa and Malik, she was afraid to leave town without them—even though that clearly made sense. She didn't want to have to fight her mother to get them back. The idea of fighting her mother made her stomach tighten. It had taken Blanche a long time to feel like her own woman, out from under Miz Cora's strong hand. Her mother had not approved of her refusal to belong to the church, her leaving Farleigh for New York, her decision to continue to do domestic work instead of being a nurse like her sister or some other mother-proud profession. They'd been fighting for nearly twenty years over Blanche's unstraightened hair. In those years, Blanche's relationship with Miz Cora had grown less contentious, as Blanche had proved that she was both moral and ungodly, that New York would not automatically make her a junkie, and that she would not be arrested as a revolutionary because of her hairdo. Still, in her mother's house, where Miz Cora's spirit seemed to be the major ingredient holding walls and floors together, Blanche sometimes felt she was once again in ankle socks and braids. She didn't intend for Taifa and Malik to have to fight so hard for their freedom. She dialed the phone again. Ardell answered on the first ring.

"Hey, girlfriend. I was just thinking about you. How'd it go this morn—What's wrong?"

Ardell's recognition that something was wrong before Blanche told her so was one of the reasons why their friendship was almost as old as they were. All through Blanche's New York years, through the year in which Blanche had lived in California as a grownup runaway, through Ardell's crazy marriage and religious conversion (and unconversion), they'd supported and encouraged each other with an intensity and constancy that had often made their men jealous and suspicious. Neither Blanche nor Ardell paid that any mind. They didn't think their relationship was anybody else's business and were both quick to say so.

"Oh, girl! You are not going to believe this shit!" Blanche proceeded to bring Ardell up to date and asked her to call the women whose houses Blanche had agreed to clean in the next few days.

"I'll tell them you got the flu. And I'll go by and see if there's anything your mama needs doing."

"That's what I really need. I feel so bad dumping all this worry on Mama and the kids, too."

"I'd be glad to keep the kids, but you know Miz Cora will rip out my jugular vein if I even suggest she part with her grand-babies! As for worry, Miz Cora has handled a whole lot worse than this! Don't you go looking for things to be upset about. You got enough on your plate." Ardell paused, then added, "I think what I really need to do is borrow a car and come get your butt!"

"No. We're leaving for their place in the country in a couple of hours. I'll be safer there. But right now, I need to get off this phone and get these people's lunch on the table." She spoke quickly and urgently, trying to cut Ardell off from where she was surely headed with her comment about borrowing a car. Blanche knew just whose car Ardell had in mind. But her effort to derail Ardell was as futile as it usually was.

"What about Leo?" Ardell's voice was a study in nonchalance that didn't fool Blanche for a second. "You want me to call him? He—"

"Don't even start it, Ardell. You know how I feel about Leo. I've told you I—"

"All right, all right," Ardell interrupted. "You just let me know how I can help."

"Thanks, honey. I'll be in touch." Blanche hung up the receiver and drummed her fingers on the counter. In a way she was grateful to Ardell for bringing up Leo. She needed something to get on her left nerve, to keep her from feeling sorry for herself or too scared to function. And there was nothing like the mention of Leo to raise her temperature.

They hadn't been a couple since high school. But some people in town, including Ardell, seemed to think they were star-crossed lovers. And she wasn't sure Leo didn't think the same thing, bringing the kids toys and games, and helping them with their homework. If a way to a man's heart was through his stomach, surely the way to a mother's heart was through her children. Unfortunately, he also offered her unsolicited advice on everything from how she should raise them to what she should wear. And as if to irritate her even more, Taifa and Malik, with prompting from no one, had taken to calling him Uncle Leo. If Blanche had ten dollars for every time she'd told him to mind his own damned business, she'd have enough money to buy a car and leave town right now. But no matter how she screamed at him, or how sarcastic she became, he was always willing to help her in whatever way she needed, even as he lectured her about being impractical and half-crazy. Maybe that was what irritated her most. It was as if he'd decided to wear her down with kindness and decency. Well, she certainly didn't want him butting his nose in now, chastising her for not having come to him for the money she needed, and treating her as though she ought to have a keeper! Fortified by her indignation over Leo, she turned to face her current situation with a bit more confidence.

Yes, there is an end to this, she told herself. I've lived through times at least as bad. Having her apartment building burn down in the heart of winter, with two kids to care for, was surely as terrible as going to jail for thirty days. Having everything that was portable stolen from her apartment and then being mugged on the street not once, not twice, but three times in as many weeks, was certainly in the same ball park as being on the run from the sheriff. I just got to be up to whatever I got to do, she told herself.

She moved around the kitchen, opening cabinets in search of plates. The first door she opened revealed shelves full of raspberry vinegar, coriander, virgin olive oil, saffron, things she'd used with regularity in the kitchens of the smart Manhattan condos and lofts, and the mellow old family-owned brownstones where she'd rented out her services as cook, housekeeper, lady's maid, housemaid, waitress, laundress, seamstress—whichever of her services, or set of services, an employer needed to buy and could afford. The kitchens she came across now that she was reduced to day work in Farleigh were more likely to be stocked with Crisco than caviar. Rich and well fed, she thought, and wondered about the people who would take the other two places at lunch. She tasted a bit of Italian pimiento, a few French capers. In other kitchens, she'd sometimes held foreign foods and imagined herself buying them in their country of origin. Sometimes, this fantasy led to the realization of how much there was to see and do in the world, and how little of it she was likely to experience. Today, she'd have traded a chance to travel the globe for the ability to simply go home.

She was distracted from the fermented beans on her fingertip by the certain knowledge that she was about to have a visitor she knew was not the blond woman. Blanche turned toward the back door. It was slowly opened by a short, plump young man with almond-shaped eyes. He wore a dark blue suit that could have been a uniform, even though he wore his pants high in the crotch and belted tightly above his belly. The belt wasn't in the belt loops. Although he wasn't all that hefty, he reminded Blanche of the Japanese sumo wrestlers she'd seen on TV late one night when she couldn't sleep for worrying about how to pay the gas bill and the electric bill with the same sixty-five dollars. His whole body was round, from the dome of his balding head (although he looked no more than twenty-five or so) to his rounded shoulders, baby paunch, and round-toed Buster Brown shoes. A black strap held a pair of glasses with clear plastic frames onto his face. One large, plump hand clutched the doorknob. There was an air of harmlessness about him that was puzzling in a white male.

"Hey." His voice was sweeter than she'd expected. She nodded. "Mumsfield," he said, thumping his chest lightly. He closed the door behind him and gave her a shy, gap-toothed smile. Blanche was partial to gap-toothed folks, having a significant space between her own front teeth.

"Blanche." She slowly screwed the lid back on the jar she was holding, but her attention was on the young man. She'd known someone was about to come through the back door, and it was him.

"I drive the car." Mumsfield hiked his pants even higher. Red-blond hairs curled on his wrists below the sleeves of his jacket. Chauffeur, Blanche thought, and continued opening cabinets.

"I am very good with automobiles." He said the last word very slowly, releasing each syllable separately, as though he hated to let it go. "Very good with automobiles," he repeated.

Conceited chauffeur, Blanche thought, and kinda country or something. She wondered why the woman hadn't given him time off like the rest of the regular help, then remembered they were going to the country after lunch. She hoped this wasn't one of those families who needed the hired help to do everything but wipe their behinds.

"This afternoon, I drive to the country house," Mumsfield told her, seeming to repeat her thought. "The country house is Aunt Emmeline's favorite place." He paused for a moment. When he spoke again his voice was even softer than before, and sadder. "Maybe Aunt Emmeline will be herself at the country house. Mumsfield...I mean, I hope so. What do you think, Blanche?"

Blanche gave him a skeptical look and wondered what the hell he was talking about. "We'll all be all right at the country house if you keep your eyes on the road and obey the speed limit," she told him.

"Oh, Blanche! You are funny, Blanche!" He had a childish giggle that made her smile.

She wanted to ask him who, besides the blond woman, would be at lunch, as well her name, but she held her questions. She was supposed to have worked for these people before. She tried a door that could have been to a large cabinet, the cellar, or another room. The door was locked.

"What's in here?"

"Cellar," he told her. "The freezer and washing machine are down there."

Probably the wine, too, she thought. Why lock up the laundry room? She opened other cabinets but didn't find any plates. Well, at least he can tell me where the plates are; I can't be expected to remember that. She was trying to decide what else she could ask him, when she found the built-in dish cabinet. She took out three plates.

"Cook let me set the table before she left, Blanche," he said. "Mumsfield...I mean I was very sad to see Cook leave." He hung his massive head, with its fringe of shiny, straight red-blond hair. Blanche was almost sure she saw his chin quiver.

"Well, she'll be back soon enough." She began removing the lunch platters from the refrigerator. She wondered if the cook was his woman. Even so, it was a bit out of the ordinary to have the chauffeur helping set the table. And why did he talk about himself as though he were someone else? Of course, a lot of these small-town Southern folks were strange, marrying their cousins and whatnot. And he was odd-looking, too. He reminded her of someone, but she didn't know who.

"Where is the country house?" she asked as nonchalantly as she could.

"Near Hokeysville, Blanche."

Blanche nodded. She didn't know the area, except that it wasn't far from the coast. It also wasn't close to a town where the interstate bus was likely to stop for passengers.

"Excuse me, Mumsfield, honey." Blanche carried a platter of sliced turkey, rare roast beef, and ham through the swinging door into the dining room. She was mindful of how thoughtlessly the word "honey" had attached itself to his name.

Blanche hadn't paid any attention to the dining room when she'd peeked in earlier. It was a high-ceilinged room papered in a deep rose with gold leaf. A long, gleaming rosewood table was surrounded by chairs with backs taller than Blanche. The towering chairs, the high, glistening sideboard, and the huge pictures of plantations and open fields were all so outsized that Blanche played with the possibility of the furniture belonging to some giant. She knew from other places she'd worked that rich people liked owning things made by different kinds of people—Africans, Eskimos, Native Americans. It didn't seem to matter what the object looked like, or to what gory purpose it might have been put, as long as it had belonged to some other people first, and as long ago as possible. So, why not a giant's things, too? She smiled as she carted iced tea, water, and coffee into the dining room. She was making up a story to tell Ardell's five-year-old niece about the giant's furniture factory.

But she wouldn't be going back to her neighborhood. She wouldn't be seeing Ardell's niece or her own children for a while. Her growing sense of having been wrenched out of her own life and plopped down in the midst of somebody else's was interrupted by a slight sound from beyond a closed door on the other side of the dining room. She turned toward it. The door was moving slowly inward. A man was speaking as he pushed the door in front of him. Blanche stepped quickly into the pantry and let the swinging door ease almost shut. She wasn't concerned that Mumsfield might catch her eavesdropping. She knew he'd left the kitchen while she was in the dining room. She noted the fact that she hadn't heard him leave, but she knew he was gone. She plastered her eye to the crack between door and frame.

The man's rugged features and sun-bleached hair were the sort associated with scoping big game in Kenya, or fishing for marlin from a cabin cruiser in the blazing Caribbean sun. Blanche expected that his smile would be dazzling. She had a personal aversion to pretty men and therefore wondered whether he had anything to offer besides a gorgeous face. Certainly the price of his very casual trousers, shirt, and jacket could have fed a family of four for six months or so.

"Grace, I tell you, it won't take more than ten minutes," he told the blond woman, who had followed him into the room. She was wringing her hands as though they were wash. He spoke to her in an affectionate "Now, now" kind of voice that set Blanche's teeth on edge. He paused to regard himself in the huge, gilt-framed mirror across the room. From the smile he gave his reflection, it seemed he had no quarrel with himself.

"You know what he's like," the man went on. "As soon as we tell him she's got a lingering cold and a bad cough, he'll move off fast enough!" He laughed and turned toward the woman. He said something about somebody's eyesight that Blanche couldn't quite make out.

"But Everett, what if she won't cooperate? She was awful to me just now! She's uncontrollable!" The man laughed, took her fluttering hands, and held them between his like captured birds. He had the kind of large, long-fingered hands Blanche's Aunt Mae always said were a sign of a man generously endowed else-where as well.

"Don't worry, darling, she'll cooperate. I promise you." He spoke softly, but some undertone in his voice made Blanche glad she wasn't the person he was talking about. Yet even as his voice chilled her, she was struck by the almost motherly way he inclined not just his head but his whole body toward Grace.

There was something in his stance that spoke of both protection and preening, as though he were not only lending his strength and protection to this nervous, worrying woman, but glorying in his ability to do so. Grace looked up at him with wide, staring eyes.

"Grace and Everett," Blanche mouthed as the couple moved out of her sight in the direction of the buffet. She didn't really care about their last names. She always called her employers by their first names in her mind. It helped her to remember that having the money to hire a domestic worker didn't make you any better than the worker, only richer. She also called her employers ma'am and sir to their faces, no matter how much they insisted on some other title or name. She'd once had two cats named Ma'am and Sir.

"Damn her anyway!" The clink of cutlery underscored his words. "If your dear aunt hadn't foolishly decided to leave the bulk of her estate to your idiot cous—"

Blanche's attention was distracted by a feeling that surprised her. Mumsfield, she thought. At that moment, he opened the same door Grace and Everett had used. What was he doing there? His hair was freshly combed and gleaming. He had on the same blue suit and white shirt, but he'd added a pair of wide, bright-orange suspenders.

"Hello, Cousin Everett. Hello, Cousin Grace," he said, and went to join them by the buffet.

"Well, I'll be damned," Blanche mouthed to herself.

"Hello, dear."

"Hello, my boy!" Everett's voice was louder than when he'd been talking to Grace, as though he thought Mumsfield had a hearing problem.

If they're his cousins, then the Aunt Emmeline Mumsfield talked about must also be one of the family, not an old family servant with an honorary title, as Blanche had thought. Maybe Aunt Emmeline was the one Grace had said was uncontrollable.

Was that why she wasn't having lunch with the rest of the family? And why was Mumsfield pretending to be the chauffeur? She remembered he hadn't really said he was the chauffeur, only that he drove the car. So much for her concern about a family unwilling to lift a finger for themselves. At least one member of the family seemed more than willing.

The three of them settled at the table: Everett at its head, Grace to his left, with her back to Blanche, and Mumsfield on his right, facing the pantry. Blanche studied him. She noticed the folds in the corner of his eyes, the thickness of his fingers. Of course, she thought. Now she remembered who he'd reminded her of earlier. It was Baby Joe, Miz Harriet's son. But Baby Joe had serious mental problems from Down's syndrome. Could you have Down's syndrome but show it only a little bit? She remembered the way Mumsfield talked about himself by name and how carefully he pronounced some words, lingering over the sounds the way children often do.

In her interest in Mumsfield, Blanche leaned a bit too heavily against the door. It swung out into the dining room. Blanche quickly pushed the door even harder and poked her head into the room, as if it had all been planned.

"Is everything all right, ma'am?"

"Oh! Oh, yes." Grace motioned Blanche to enter the room. Everett lunged for and caught the glass Grace nearly toppled. Two big drops of water splashed onto her rare roast beef. Everett fussed over her plate and insisted on getting her another helping. Blanche took the watered roast beef away and brought a clean plate. Everett filled it and took it to Grace.

"Everett, Mumsfield, this is...er...this is...the woman the agency sent. She's worked for us before." Grace avoided making eye contact with Everett.

Mumsfield gave Blanche a quizzical look. He opened his mouth as if to speak, then shut it again.

"Yes, sir," Blanche said quickly. "I'm glad to be back working for ya'll again." She glanced quickly at Mumsfield. He gave her a Cheshire Cat smile.

"Her first name is Blanche, Cousin Grace," he said. "I don't remember her last name." He winked at Blanche before turning his attention to the huge mound of potato salad on his plate.

"White is my last name," Blanche added in a clear, assertive tone. "Blanche White."

The moment it was out, she could have kicked herself for not making up a phony name. It was her family's fault for giving her a name that made her so defensive she hadn't even thought to lie to these people. She watched surprise turn to a barely concealed grin on Everett's face. Grace looked startled. Blanche could tell from her arm movements that she was twisting her napkin in her lap. Mumsfield stopped eating to look from Grace to Everett, as though their faces would tell him what was happening that he didn't understand.

Blanche was accustomed to some people getting the chuckles when they heard her name. She didn't think having a name that meant "white" twice was any funnier than a woman who tripped over invisible objects and knocked over water glasses being called Grace. Blanche gave them a curt nod and returned to the kitchen.

She was waiting for Mumsfield when he opened the back door.

"I know everyone who has ever worked in our kitchen," he told her with obvious pride. "First there was Evie, then Clara, then Bea, then…" He went on to name the various cooks and kitchen help who'd been a part of the household. When he'd finished, he gave her an expectant look.

"Thanks for not telling on me," Blanche told him. "They won't let me stay if they know I haven't worked here before, and I really need the job." She fought the urge to tell him about her kids and to make up a sick parent to go with them.

"I can keep a secret, Blanche," he announced, as though he recognized that keeping a secret was a rare ability. He gave her a jaunty wave and a smile that scrunched all his features into the middle of his face. He was out the back door before she could thank him again. She was surprised by her own certainty that he could be trusted, at least on this issue.

Mumsfield had been gone about ten minutes when her next visitor showed up. Grace poked her head into the kitchen while Blanche was putting away the last of the lunch dishes.

"Are you ready, er...ah...Blanche?"

"Yes, ma'am." Woman stumbles over my name like a shoe on the stairs, Blanche huffed to herself. But at least Grace hadn't reminded her to call the agency. Blanche hung the dish towel on the rack and picked up her handbag from the chair. She followed Grace through the dining room and down a long hall to the very front of the house. The hollow sound of their footfalls on the black and white marble floor seemed to scurry away to explore the distant corners of the large, cold space. She was aware that every place she'd ever lived could fit into this one marble warehouse. But why would anyone want a room where hard-seated chairs weren't even within shouting distance of one another? She pictured the forest green crushed-velvet living-room suite with the round chaise longue and copper studs down the sides of the sofa that she'd been drooling over in Lassiter's Fine Furniture Mart window. She never ceased to marvel over the ways rich people spent their money.

Blanche was staring up at the cupids painted on the ceiling when the hair at the nape of her neck rose to attention. She turned and watched Everett coming toward her. He was pushing a wheelchair. The woman in the chair was asleep. Her dirty white sausage curls bobbed gently, like the head of the felt and plaster hound dog in the back window of Blanche's cousin Buddy's car.

Old thing looks like she invented wrinkles, Blanche thought. She wore a short-sleeved pink and green floral-print dress of the simple, very expensive variety. A white angora shawl rested on her shoulders and a dark green lap robe covered her lower body. She had about a quarter of a pound of rice powder on her face. "You remember Aunt Emmeline," Grace whispered to Blanche, who nodded in the affirmative.

Everett wheeled the chair ahead of them to the front door. "I'm afraid she's feeling poorly again." Grace continued to whisper. Blanche gave Grace what she hoped was a sympathetic, understanding look and followed her outside.

A long black limousine, made even darker by its tinted windows, was waiting for them at the bottom of the wide front stairs. There was a freshly painted wooden ramp to the left of the stairs. Mumsfield stood by the car, the back passenger door open. He bounced eagerly on the balls of his feet. He'd changed his orange suspenders for jonquil yellow ones. He didn't seem to know what to do with his hands, which alternately waved at Emmeline and dived into his jacket pockets. Everett wheeled Emmeline across the porch toward the ramp. Mumsfield walked quickly toward the old lady. His face was in full smile, his arms open in pre-hug position. Grace hurried forward and laid a restraining hand on Mumsfield's arm. "Now, dear, you don't want to give Aunt Em any more of those nasty germs, do you?"

Blanche had to stop herself from sucking her teeth in disgust. What bunk! The boy didn't even have a cold. She gave Emmeline a piercing look. Was she one of those ignorant, superstitious people bred and raised to believe that any kind of difference is revolting? It was certainly common in Emmeline's generation of Americans, both up and down South.

As though sensing in her sleep that she was the center of attention, Aunt Emmeline stirred in her chair. She raised her head and turned it slowly from side to side. "Hello, everybody! Hello!" she called out in a husky, shaky voice through lips covered with poorly applied bright red lipstick. She nodded and waved. Like she's queen of the Fourth of July parade, Blanche chuckled to herself. No wonder Mumsfield misses her company. She's the liveliest one of the bunch.

Everett leaned forward and whispered something in the old lady's ear. She gave him an unreadable look and sat back in her chair. Grace took Mumsfield's arm and inched him back toward the car.

"Come along, Blanche." Grace climbed into the back seat of the car and closed the door firmly behind her. While Blanche was fastening her seat belt, there was a soft whirring from behind. She turned her head and watched a glass partition rising between the front and back seats.

Mumsfield handled the car like a loving parent guiding a favorite child. The car moved forward as though cushioned on a cloud. Lord! If that stuck-up Helen Robinson could see me now! Blanche grinned to herself and pressed her feet a little deeper into the plush carpeting. She ran her hand across the glove-leather seat. Money, she thought. It ain't even real, not like dirt or grass. But if you don't have any...She turned her head slightly and peeked at the three people in the back seat, people so different from her they might as well have been two-headed or made of glass, people who'd never once in their entire lives had to worry about the cost of groceries, paying their rent, or whether they had enough money to buy medicine for a sick child. What must it feel like? she wondered.

A passing County Sheriff's Department car reminded her that she had more than money to worry about. She began to slip lower in her seat, then realized the law would no more look for her in a car like this than they would expect to find her in a convent. A fiery shaft of summer sun, in an otherwise cloudy sky, flashed through the trees and bounced off a highway sign. A good omen, she decided.

THREE

The country house sat on a rise overlooking a duck pond. A huge bed of pink, white, and yellow flowers lay on the far side of the pond, between the pond and the pinewood forest that seemed to ring the whole property. The highway was totally invisible. Not even the noise of passing cars and trucks could be heard. The briny smell of the sea in the air told her they'd crossed that invisible border between inland and shore. The pine trees whispered about their arrival.

The house was nowhere near the size of the house in town. This was a wooden house, painted a lavender-gray made even more delicate by the deep green of the grass and the pine trees around it. A screened porch extended around three sides of the house. White wicker chairs and small tables were placed casually around the porch and added to the touches of white that framed the doors and windows and shimmered on the wheelchair ramp. The gabled roof and woodland setting made Blanche think of fairy tales. But the house didn't have a fairy-tale air. The house was anxious, as though something of which it did not approve had taken place on its premises, or was about to. Blanche wondered if it was her arrival or something else. She rooted for something else. There could be no harder task than working in a house that didn't like you. For as long as she was here, she needed to keep a very low profile. She hoped the house would cooperate.

Blanche lined up behind the members of the family as they filed up the short ramp to the front porch. Grace was once again careful to keep Mumsfield away from the old lady in the wheelchair.

The inside of the house was cozier than the house in town: deep sofas and big old rattan chairs with rose chintz covers and cushions, worn leather hassocks, dark green woven rugs, and large photographs of people in old-fashioned dress on the white-washed walls.

Grace took Blanche up the back stairs to a small room furnished with a single bed, a four-drawer dresser, a bedside table, a lamp, and a straight-backed chair. Murky-brown linoleum covered the floor, the same linoleum she'd encountered in many such rooms. No doubt there was a store somewhere that specialized in murky-brown linoleum and scratchy sheets for the help. "It's a pleasant enough little room, don't you think?" Grace had the nerve to say.

"Well, it ain't going to spoil me, that's for sure," Blanche told her. She might have to sleep in this mousehole, but she'd be damned if she'd act grateful.

Grace chose not to address the issue. "I'll be waiting in the kitchen when you've changed." She closed the door firmly behind her.

The room overlooked the back garden, the shed at its foot, and the pinewoods beyond. There was an older black man in a baseball cap working in the vegetable garden.

True to Grace's prediction, in the shallow clothes closet there were two washed and starched gray uniforms with white collars and cuffs and small white aprons to match. Blanche was delighted to find they were a size sixteen. Wearing clothes a size too big always made her feel slim. When she'd changed into one of the uniforms, she found her way down to the kitchen. Grace was waiting for her. Grace wasn't exactly frowning, but her face was tense. She seemed to be holding herself in readiness for a loud noise or bad news. When she saw Blanche, she immediately began discussing meals.

"A small porterhouse, for my aunt's dinner. Perhaps some potatoes, or…" Grace paused, as though her train of thought had been derailed by a more compelling message from some side track of her brain. Blanche waited and wondered about the advisability of a porterhouse steak for an ailing elderly lady.

"There will be a guest at dinner, just one," Grace went on at last. She fiddled with the small pen and leather-covered notebook on the table in front of her. "He likes simple food. Roast chicken, I think. We eat promptly at seven-thirty. Promptly. I don't like Mr. Everett, my husband, to be kept waiting."

Grace said the words "my husband" like a new bride still dazzled by the idea. Blanche felt a surge of dislike for the man. Too rich to wait, she thought, too rich, too white, too male. And too pampered by his wife.

"Aunt will want her dinner around five. I'll take it up myself if you'll just let me know when it's ready. She prefers that I bring her meals," she explained. She didn't sound as pleased about catering to her aunt as to her husband.

"Now, then…" Grace opened her notebook and went over the menus for the next five days, then gave Blanche the phone number for the grocery store in Hokeysville.

An hour after Blanche phoned, a sweaty, red-faced boy delivered the four bags of groceries she'd ordered. He gave Blanche the cheeky "Hey, girl" greeting that teenage white boys working up to being full-fledged rednecks give grown black women in the South. Blanche hissed some broken Swahili and Yoruba phrases she'd picked up at the Freedom Library in Harlem and told the boy it was a curse that would render his penis as slim and sticky as a lizard's tongue. The look on his face and the way he clutched his crotch lifted her spirits considerably. Nina Simone's version of "I Put a Spell on You" came rolling out of her mouth in a deep, off-key grumble. She ran a carrot through the food processor until it was a pile of thin orange coins. She washed a baking potato and once again wondered why the old lady wasn't having soup or scrambled eggs. If she was up to eating a hearty meal, why wasn't she having dinner with the family? She steamed the carrots, put the steak on the grill, and readied the potato for the microwave. When the tray was ready, she went looking for Grace.

Blanche hesitated in the doorway to the living room, struck by the realization that this was the first time she'd seen Grace motionless. Grace's head rested against the back of a large, old-fashioned rattan armchair. There was a haughtiness in her profile that wasn't noticeable when she was in motion. Her hands were loosely folded in her lap. She seemed to be looking out the window, toward the duck pond, but Blanche was sure whatever Grace was really seeing wasn't going on outside. Her stillness was so deep, so unblinking, she might have been in a trance. But there was something burning in the back of her eyes when she turned her head and looked at Blanche.

If Grace had been a friend, Blanche would have immediately asked what was troubling her. But she'd long ago learned the painful price of confusing the skills she sold for money with the kind of caring that could be paid for only with reciprocity.

"You're looking a little peaked, ma'am. You want me to take the tray up?" She let an edge of concern creep into her voice. It was a tone she used when inviting her employers to provide anecdotal evidence that money was indeed not everything.

"I know I should take it up myself, but…"

"Caring for old folks can be a trial sometimes." Blanche commiserated.

Grace looked at her for a long moment, then lowered her head. "She's changed a lot in the last…since the last time you saw her." She fiddled with her fingers. Blanche waited for her to continue.

"That's why I especially asked for someone who knew her before, someone who'd remember what a sweet, sweet dear she was before…" Her voice got snagged on something in her throat.

She covered her eyes with her right hand. "You'll see what I mean."

Blanche hesitated. She didn't want to walk in on the old lady doing anything disgusting. Or dangerous.

"She's not violent, is she, ma'am?"

"Oh, no. Nothing like that. It's..." She covered her face and sobbed softly for a few minutes. Finally she raised her head and looked at Blanche.

Blanche was unimpressed by the tears, and Grace's Mammy-save-me eyes. Mammy-savers regularly peeped out at her from the faces of some white women for whom she worked, and lately, in this age of the touchy-feely model of manhood, an occasional white man. It happened when an employer was struck by family disaster or grew too compulsive about owning everything, too overwrought, or downright frightened by who and what they were. She never ceased to be amazed at how many white people longed for Aunt Jemima. They'd ease into the kitchen and hem and haw their way through some sordid personal tale. She'd listen and make sympathetic noises. She rarely asked questions, except to clarify the life lessons their stories conveyed, or to elicit some detail that would make their story more amusing to her friends. She told employers who asked what she would do in their place, or what she thought they ought to do, "I sure wish I knew, I truly do," accompanied by a slow, sad smile, a matching shake of her head, and arms folded tightly across her chest.

Now Blanche knew that if she went to Grace, put her hand on the woman's shoulder, and looked concerned, it was likely Grace would bare the family soul. But Blanche didn't yet know whether Grace was the kind of person who both longed for someone on whom to unburden herself and was then grateful to the listener, or the kind of person who resented the listener for catching her at a weak moment. She took a half-step forward, hesitated, then crossed the room to where Grace sat.

"Is there anything I can do, ma'am?" Whether she cared or not, there were certain expected forms to be observed.

"No, no." Grace continued to sob but made no attempt to talk.

"I'll take the tray up now, ma'am."

Blanche went back to the kitchen for the tray and carried it up the stairs. She was both curious and concerned about what awaited her in the old lady's room. At the top of the staircase she realized she hadn't asked Grace which room was Emmeline's. The one farthest from the back stairs and overlooking the front of the house and the duck pond seemed like the right room for the family member with the money. Blanche was sure Emmeline fit that description. She'd worked in so many wealthy households she recognized the mix of respect, hate, and hope that crept into family members' voices when they talked about the moneyed one.

"I brought your dinner, ma'am," Blanche called from outside the door when there was no response to her knock. She balanced the tray on her left hip and reached for the doorknob.

"I'm coming in now." And I'm going to feel like a damned fool if I've been talking to an empty room, she added to herself. She turned the knob and pushed the door.

Emmeline was lolling on a pale green brocade wing chair. A matching ottoman propped up her stockinged feet. A water glass with a small amount of clear liquid in it hung loosely from her right hand. She wore the same dress she'd worn on the ride from town. Only now the front was littered with cigarette ashes. The dress was also rucked well up her legs. Pink garters made tight rings above her lumpy red knees. Her thighs seemed to be melting off her bones and spreading in puddles on the chair around her. She was staring at a large color TV on which an excited-looking woman held up a can of Zesto! floor wax and moved her lips. The sound was turned too low to hear what she was saying. The small, round table by Emmeline's side held a porcelain ashtray overflowing with ashes and butts. The tablecloth was spotted with dark rings. The air in the room was thick with smoke and the smell of stale booze and not quite clean feet. Blanche was struck by the difference between Emmeline and her surroundings. She looked like a drunken Little Orphan Annie at eighty, with her frizzy yellow-white hair and blank, watery eyes. The room, on the other hand, was neat and bright, the kind of genteel room that she imagined a woman who read romantic historical novels and did needlepoint might have. Liquor sure does funny things to people, she thought.

"I brought you some dinner, ma'am."

"Don't give me that 'brought you some dinner' crap, gal. I know they sent you to spy on me!"

Blanche opened her mouth to tell Emmeline that her name was Blanche, not gal, then thought better of it. She set the tray on the bed while she made space for it on the table at Emmeline's side. When she looked around for the wastebasket, she spotted a rolling table of the kind hospitals use to serve meals to bed-ridden patients, only better looking. She gave Emmeline a why-didn't-you-tell-me look. Emmeline's lips curled in a mean-spirited smile. Blanche set the tray on the rolling table, lowered it to armchair height, and wheeled it within Emmeline's easy reach.

"Would you like anything else, ma'am?"

Emmeline reached down and lifted a bottle of Seagram's gin from beneath the floor-length tablecloth, filled her glass, and returned her bottle to its resting place. Blanche eased the door closed behind her as she left the room.

Now she understood why Mumsfield was being kept away from his aunt. Blanche wondered what had started Emmeline drinking. Boredom, maybe. She'd worked for or around a number of rich old ladies like that—lots of money, no friends, no interests to speak of. Perfect candidates for an alcohol problem. But were Grace and Everett really stupid enough to think they could keep it from Mumsfield indefinitely?

In the kitchen, she checked her rising rolls before cleaning the chickens. She was glad for Grace's dinner order of roast chicken, julienned string beans, scalloped potatoes, rolls, and apple pie with ice cream. A more elaborate meal would have called for more concentration than she could muster today.

She searched the chickens for missed feathers, squeezed out a few overlooked shafts, and singed off the fine feathers on the wings before reaching her hand into the chicken's cool, slick body cavity to yank out the few unsavory bits left behind by the original cleaner. But although she was thorough and worked efficiently, her mind was preoccupied with when and how to head for New York.

The idea of moving the children back to New York made her stomach lurch. At the same time, New York was the one place she knew she could find work quickly among people who wouldn't ask questions about paying her in cash or balk at her use of a different name. She was sure the good people of Farleigh weren't going to spend too many tax dollars on hunting for her. Unless, of course, they took her escape as a personal affront to all decent, God-fearing white people. She remembered the wanted posters for Joanne Little, Angela Davis, and Assata Shakur. She blushed at putting herself in such important company, then wondered if the sheriff's office appreciated the distinction. She silently apologized to any heavyset black women the sheriff's men might harass because of her. She rinsed, dried, and seasoned the chickens inside and out and sat them upright on paper towels.

"I need some money," she whispered aloud. That was her first problem. She washed the chicken fat from her hands. The ninety-two dollars and change she had would get her and the kids to New York, but it wouldn't do much more than that. She could probably borrow a bit more but not enough. As it was, she was going to have to ask her friend Yvonne to put her and the kids up until she got on her feet. It was a lot to ask, but she'd once done the same for Yvonne and her three children. Blanche was suddenly conscious that somewhere above her there was a room where Grace's handbag hung on the back of a chair, or lay on a bed or bureau. Everett's wallet, too, perhaps. She pictured herself tiptoeing into that room, taking twenties, fifties, hundred-dollar bills from designer wallets and stuffing the bills in her bra. She watched herself tiptoe back down the stairs into the kitchen. In all her years of working in people's houses, she had yet to steal any money. She'd borrowed some rice or a couple of potatoes now and again, as necessity demanded, but always replaced them. She wasn't against stealing from this sort. A lot of what they owned really belonged to people like her, who were grossly and routinely underpaid, who worked in the factories and mills and made the money for the big boys. She just didn't believe in taking big risks for nickels and dimes. She also didn't want to be as cutthroat as the people she complained about. But just supposing she could make herself do it, then what? What happened when they found the money was gone? They'd have the cops on her in a flash, especially if she took off after stealing the money. And if they caught her, she'd be worse off than she was now.

But even if she wasn't prepared to steal it, she needed more money. There was her income-tax check, of course, but its arrival date was uncertain. Ardell had already gotten her refund, and they'd filed on the same day. So, maybe in a couple of days. Maybe even tomorrow. I'll need to get it, sign it....

And when she had money, how was she going to tell Taifa and Malik that despite her promise to them, and to herself, she was leaving town without them? What could she tell them that would make that all right? And how was she going to keep them from hating her and acting out in ways that might hurt them? She sagged against the sink and stared out the window into the surrounding pine trees as though they might tell her what she should do. If they knew, they weren't saying. They just went right on whispering among themselves. Blanche sighed and reached for the potatoes on the counter beside her. She halted just as her right hand was half an inch from the bright orange colander that held them. Mumsfield, she thought. In the next second he opened the back door.

This was the second or third time this boy had been on her wavelength. This thing with him was beyond her Approaching Employer Warning sense, which alerted her to the slightest rustling or clinking of a nearing employer. This was more like the way she always knew when her mother was around, or Ardell, or which one of the children was about to fling open the door and bound through the house. This ability to sense Mumsfield's approach was of the same nature but different. What made it different was the fact that she didn't know this boy and didn't appreciate having him on her frequency. At the same time, it was always those closest and kindest to her whose presence she was able to detect before they came into sight or earshot. So what the hell does it mean? She wanted to know. Sympa. It was a term her Haitian friend Marie Claire used to explain relationships between people who, on the surface, had no business being friends. Still, an unknown white boy?

Mumsfield's "Hello" was spoken so softly, Blanche might have missed it if she hadn't seen his lips move. He closed the door behind him and immediately began pacing the kitchen floor, huffing and mumbling to himself until the air in the room was as stiff as well-beaten egg whites. His pants were once again held up by a belt. Blanche wanted to ask him what had happened to his yellow suspenders, and the orange ones that had preceded them, but he was clearly too upset to discuss fashion.

"Mumsfield, honey, you gonna have to find a better way to express yourself than by bad-vibing this kitchen when I'm in here trying to cook!"

"Yes, Blanche," he mumbled. He stopped pacing but began twisting from side to side, like an agitator in a washing machine.

"Mumsfield, honey, please! Relax!" Blanche wiped her hands on her apron and beckoned to him to take a seat. She rubbed and gently kneaded his shoulders and the back of his neck, the way she did for her kids when they had nightmares. She willed the tension to leave his body and could feel his knotted muscles relaxing beneath her fingers. Once again, she was surprised by the familiarity with which she treated him, but it felt all right.

"Mumsfield is very upset." His words stumbled over each other.

"What about, Mumsfield, honey?"

"Why couldn't Mumsfield talk to her, Blanche?"

"Who, honey?"

"Why is she not the same as before, Blanche? Why is Aunt Em not the same?" He twisted around to look up into her face. "When is she going to be the same again, Blanche?" Tears glistened in his eyes.

Blanche didn't know what to say. He reminded her of Uncle Benny. Uncle Benny had a real bad stutter. Because people either ignored him or grew impatient before he could say his piece, Uncle Benny used as few words as possible. But something about the way he tilted his head or moved his hands or twisted his mouth pumped Uncle Benny's few words full of meanings and explanations that never came out directly.

"Aunt Grace says Aunt Emmeline doesn't want to see Mumsfield...me until she's all better. When will she be better, Blanche? I didn't mean to make her sick." He turned his head and gave Blanche another pained look.

"You didn't make her sick, honey. What ails her ain't hardly your fault! I'm sure she'll be all right in a couple days, and then you can have a nice long visit." Blanche figured Grace and Everett were just keeping Mumsfield away from the old lady until her binge was over. Which was why Grace had fed him that stupid germ business. Why didn't they just tell him the truth? Anyone could see how sensitive the boy was.

"But when she fell and broke her leg, she wasn't different. She let Mumsfield carry her to the car before the ramp was ready, and bring her flowers, and talk to her about when she was a girl and there were horses and buggies and no cars, and about Uncle Elmo. He said it would be all right soon, but when, Blanche? When?"

"Who said?" Blanche wanted to know.

Mumsfield put his hand over his mouth and shook his head vehemently from side to side. Before Blanche could press him, someone knocked on the back door.

"Hey, Mist' Mumsfield. Excuse me, ma'am." This time the grocery delivery boy lowered his eyes as he spoke to her and hesitated in the doorway until she motioned him inside. She was impressed with how quickly he'd learned. She'd have to remember to use her curse number more often.

"It's Mr. Mumsfield here I need to see." He turned toward Mumsfield. "The truck conked out on me down the road there. Could you maybe take a look at it?"

"Sure, Jimmy." Mumsfield wiped his eyes on the backs of his hands and bounced out of his chair as though he'd already forgotten what they'd been talking about. "I'll be right back!" He ran up the back stairs. When he returned, he had removed his jacket and was carrying a tool kit. He'd also added a pair of bright red suspenders to his attire. "I'll be back, Blanche. I trust you, Blanche," he told her.

Blanche shook her head. She wasn't interested in being trusted just now. Somehow it made her responsible, like when her kids began a question with "Now tell me the truth, Mama Blanche." She knew right off that she was about to be asked something she'd rather not answer at all but was now duty bound to answer as honestly as she could. And she always felt she ought to stick by the people who trusted her. She didn't need anybody to feel loyal to right now, especially someone like Mumsfield.

Blanche had never suffered from what she called Darkies' Disease. There was a woman among the regular riders on the bus she often rode home from work who had a serious dose of the disease. Blanche actually cringed when the woman began talking in her bus-inclusive voice about old Mr. Stanley, who said she was more like a daughter to him than his own child, and how little Edna often slipped and called her Mama. That woman and everyone else on the bus knew what would happen to all that close family feeling if she told Mr. Stanley, or little Edna's mama, that instead of scrubbing the kitchen floor she was going to sit down with a cup of coffee and make some phone calls.

Loving the people for whom you worked might make it easier to wipe old Mr. Stanley's shitty behind and take young Edna's smart-ass, rich-kid remarks. And, of course, it was hard not to love children, or to overlook the failings of the old and infirm. They were not yet responsible in the first case and beyond it in the other. What she didn't understand was how you convinced yourself that you were actually loved by people who paid you the lowest possible wages; who never offered you the use of one of their cars, their cottage by the lake, or even their swimming pool; who gave you handkerchiefs and sachets for holiday gifts and gave their children stocks and bonds. It seemed to her that this was the real danger in looking at customers through love-tinted glasses. You had to pretend that obvious facts—facts that were like fences around your relationship—were not true. Mumsfield was a grown white man in whose home she was presently hiding from the police. Still, he seemed far more capable of causing an attack of dreaded Darkies' Disease than any other person for whom she'd worked. She wondered if her heightened awareness of him might have something to do with his child self being so close to the surface. He seemed to approach the world, and her, with a trusting innocence that was both endearing and disarming. He was gentle as baby's breath, and smart enough about some things, including recognizing her as an intelligent, knowledgeable person, something the majority of her employers seemed to miss.

She pressed her hand to her chest as though it were possible to collapse that hollow feeling inside, the one that let her know when something was going on in a household. Sometimes it was a pending divorce, or a terminal illness. Sometimes it was madness or cruelty. In this case, maybe it was just Emmeline's drinking. But the hollowness in her chest was more serious than that. She could feel it in the house, too, a kind of dour restlessness. Like it's waiting for the worst to happen, she thought. Just like Grace. She reached up and turned on the radio on the windowsill over the sink. She found some soft rock to temporarily sweeten the place.

An hour before dinner she went up the back stairs to get Emmeline's tray. She steeled herself for another encounter with the woman, only to find the tray sitting on the hall table at the top of the main stairs. The meal was more picked over than eaten. Blanche leaned against the table and slipped off her left shoe. She bent down and gently rubbed the corn on her little toe. A car door slammed out in front of the house. A few moments later the front door opened and she heard someone talking in the hall below. She moved closer to the top of the stairs and closed her eyes so she could hear better. It was Everett.

"I assure you, old man, she'll be quite herself before long.... resting just now. Needs as much rest as she can get. The cough, you know, she's been keep..." Everett's voice grew fainter as he moved into the sitting room.

Rumble, mumble "...not contagious, I hope," someone replied in a deep, slow voice.

So they're trying to cover up the old drunk's binge by pretending she's sick to their guest, too. She leaned down to massage her toe again. Why did they invite this guy while Emmeline's in her cups? Maybe the conversation she'd just heard was really a piece of politeness in which everyone was pretending not to know the obvious. After all, alcoholism wasn't all that easy to hide. She thought about her own Aunt Daisy.

When Aunt Daisy took up the bottle as a serious vocation, she'd put out the story that she was drinking a fifth of port a day on her doctor's advice. "To build up my blood," she'd tell anyone brazen enough to ask. One day, she'd fallen down the front porch stairs and was too drunk to get up, just as Reverend Brown was passing by. That evening, Uncle Dan had locked Aunt Daisy in the attic until she'd dried out, thin blood or no thin blood. He'd told all the neighbors Aunt Daisy was just too weak with anemia to come out or to have any visitors. Blanche marveled at the many ways families insisted on acting the same, regardless of color or other differences.

Usually, Blanche hated waiting on table and being treated like just another utensil. But this evening she was disappointed when Grace told her she needn't stand duty in the dining room. She was curious about this guest. She couldn't recall exactly what Everett had said about him at lunch, but it had revolved around the lie that Emmeline had the flu and something taking only ten minutes. She'd looked him over as closely as she'd dared when Grace rang for more rolls. At least she'd learned his name, Archibald. He looked like a Hollywood version of a Southern gentleman: snow-white hair, glowing pink skin, and the kind of face people she'd worked for called Roman. Blanche understood this to mean a high forehead, a big nose, and no lips to speak of. While she was in the room, conversation either stopped or was nicey-nice talk.

After dinner, she carried the coffee tray into the sitting room, a small, bright room, across the hall from the living room, done in yellow and lime green wallpaper with chair cushions to match. An open liquor cabinet stood against the far wall. The furniture was white, with curved and carved arms and legs. Everett and his guest stood by the window. They were deep in conversation that only they could hear. Grace wasn't there and neither was Mumsfield. Blanche began pouring their coffee, but Everett dismissed her with a flip of his wrist.

She took her time doing the dishes. She searched for some news on the radio, but all she could find was a hillbilly whining and picking his banjo, and some rock and roll. When she turned the radio off, the songs of frogs and crickets and other night creatures seeped between the clink of the knives and forks as she washed and rinsed. It was her favorite time of summer evening. Light slipped over the horizon a few minutes before the dark took hold and created a small space between night and day where every object, every feeling, seemed starkly clear. She saw herself standing halfway between where she'd been and where she was headed. Part of her longed for Farleigh, a snatch of Taifa and Malik's bedtime bickering, the smell of their just-washed skin and milky breath. Part of her was already gone on the bus to New York, preparing for life in the city. Grace's entrance distracted Blanche from her thoughts.

"When Nate, who looks after the garden and grounds, arrives," Grace told her, "we'll be going up to Aunt Emmeline's room. We'll need you both." Grace's face was slightly flushed. "There's something I, that is, my husband and I...It will only take a mo..."

A soft sound came from the back door, something between a knock and scratching. Blanche opened it to a short, wiry old man whose skin reminded her of some deep red-black wood polished to a high sheen. He was clutching a grungy baseball cap and bobbing and weaving like a punchdrunk fighter. His denim overalls were faded to a watery blue. He gave Blanche a brief nod and slipped by her into the kitchen. She recognized him as the person she'd seen in the garden. Now she watched him bow and scrape and "Miz Grace" all around the kitchen until the object of his ass-kissing led them up the back stairs. If it's a put-on, he ought to be in the movies, Blanche thought. If it's for real, it's pitiful.

On the way upstairs, Grace kept up a constant trickle of questions and comments about the garden and the weather and the ducks on the pond. She and Nate laughed together over little remarks that meant nothing to Blanche. She did notice that Grace was wringing her hands as though she were hoping to get gold out of them. The hollow laughter of a TV laugh track seeped from beneath a bedroom door that Blanche bet was Mumsfield's.

The smell of cheap liquor and cigarettes had been replaced in Emmeline's room by the pungent fragrance of eucalyptus. A humidifier sent a jet of mist into the overheated room. Emmeline was hiked up on a mass of creamy white pillows edged with pink embroidered roses. Her blue satin bed jacket was trimmed with white lace. A matching cap covered her Little Orphan Annie Afro. Her eyes were red-rimmed but keen. She observed her visitors from over a linen handkerchief she held to her nose and mouth.

"Why, Miz Em, it sure is good to see you!" Nate performed a kind of jerky bow as he moved beyond the foot of the bed until he was near Emmeline's side. Blanche hung back, watching from just inside the door.

"I sure am sorry to see you feeling sss...sss...so..." Nate stuttered and stumbled through telling Emmeline how sorry he was that she was ill. Emmeline clutched her handkerchief closer to her face and seemed to shrink into her pillows. She flashed her eyes at Grace. Grace opened her mouth and reached out her hand to Nate, but whatever she intended was forestalled by a knock on the door. Everett ushered Archibald into the room.

"Cousin Archibald." Emmeline spoke in a high, sweet whisper that was very different from the bitchy whiskey rasp Blanche had heard earlier.

Archibald crossed the room to the far side of the bed and set his briefcase on the table by the window. He took the hand Emmeline held out to him.

"Cousin." He bowed low over Emmeline's hand. His silver hair gleamed in the light from the window. "You can't know how much it means to me that you asked to see me, personally, after so long. I..."

Emmeline lowered her handkerchief and coughed a quick succession of loud barks in Archibald's direction. He flinched and took a quick step back from the bed. "Don't try to talk, my dear."

Emmeline coughed again. Archibald snatched his own handkerchief from his breast pocket and brought it quickly to his mouth and nose. After a few moments, his eyes widened and crimson crept up to his forehead. He looked quickly down at Emmeline, who was once again hidden behind her handkerchief. By the time he shifted his gaze to see if Grace and Everett had noticed, he had already stuffed the offending handkerchief back in its proper place. Blanche saw laughter in Emmeline's eyes.

Archibald opened his briefcase. The minute she saw that sheath of heavy, thick, clothlike paper, Blanche knew they were there about money. Archibald fussed with his papers while Everett fetched the rolling tray from the other side of the room. He pushed it to the bed so that it extended across Emmeline's lap.

"I really do hate to bother you, Cousin, but you did insist that I come today." Archibald laid the papers on the tray in front of Emmeline. "If you'll just sign here." He used his pen as a pointer.

Emmeline lowered her handkerchief and produced a series of loud, dry coughs. This time, Emmeline wasn't the only cougher. Blanche had to manufacture a cough of her own to cover the grin that sprang unbidden to her face when Archibald practically threw the pen on the tray and jumped away from the bed as though his life depended upon putting distance between himself and his cousin.

Blanche was now positive Emmeline was making mischief. She tried to catch Nate's eye, to see if he'd noticed it, too, but he had eyes only for the baseball cap he was squeezing to death between both hands.

Emmeline was reading through the four or five sheets of paper Archibald had given her. She ran her eyes down each page in a leisurely fashion, then picked it up and turned it face down on the tray with slow, deliberate movements before going on to the next page. Every once in a while she coughed into the handkerchief she still held to her mouth. Warning shots, Blanche thought. The air in the room was as charged as a thunderstorm.

"It's a wise change, if I may say so." Archibald cleared his throat. "All the other items, of course, remain the same." Archibald moved a tad closer to his cousin. His eyes seemed to implore her not to infect him any more than she'd already done. "The bequests to the servants, the generous gift to the Daughters of the Confederacy…"

He petered out as the old lady continued to read, or at least pretended to read.

Grace was breathing through her mouth in short, quick bursts. Her hands were white-knuckled fists at her side. Everett lay his hand on the small of Grace's back for just a moment. She gave him a poor excuse for a smile, but Everett never took his eyes off Emmeline.

There was a light coating of sweat on Everett's forehead. And Blanche could almost feel Nate concentrating on the baseball cap in his hands. Did Emmeline's teasing Archibald account for all the tension bunched in the room? Blanche doubted it.

"Of course, I agree with you," Archibald said, as though responding to something Emmeline had said. "Mumsfield's a fine lad, a clever boy…all things considered. But managing an estate as large as yours is a complicated business. Better to have older, more…er…ah…capable members of the family in charge of his affairs." He smiled over at Everett and Grace.

"The firm is at your service," he told them. "And, of course, I personally will be glad to—"

He was cut off by a hacking cough from Emmeline. He stepped back until his butt bumped against his briefcase on the table behind him. Emmeline snatched up the pen and signed the last page, coughing as she wrote. Blanche felt rather than heard a collective sigh from Grace and Everett. Archibald looked a little

49

shocked. Was it the old lady's quickness with the pen that surprised him?

He grabbed the will before Emmeline could cough on it again. He held it gingerly, as though it were one of those smallpox blankets the early settlers gave to the Indians. Blanche half expected him to whip out a pair of rubber gloves. He laid the last page on the table beside his briefcase and motioned Blanche and Nate closer. He handed the pen to Blanche and pointed to a line beneath Emmeline's signature. Blanche wished she'd said she couldn't write. But at least it didn't sound as though Mumsfield was being cut out of his money, only having it handled by his cousins. Blanche wrote her name in a round, girlish hand on the line next to Archibald's manicured pink-white finger. It occurred to her that just because Mumsfield's cousins were handling his money was no reason to assume his money was safe. Archibald took the pen from her and handed it to Nate. Nate leaned stiffly over the table and signed his name in shaky script.

"I'd like to stay and chat, Cousin, but I can see that you need your rest." Archibald stuffed the pen and the will in his briefcase and moved quickly toward the door. Emmeline coughed again, as if to hurry him along. Everett followed him out of the room.

Grace dismissed Nate with a nod and a vague smile, and told Blanche that Everett would lock up. Nate followed Blanche down the back stairs.

"What do you make of all that?" Blanche asked him.

"I sure wisht I wasn't in it." His eyes looked older than dirt. His shoulders drooped. "You ain't from round here, is you?" He gave Blanche a searching look that took in her hair, and her feet, and all in between. Including, she thought, some parts that don't show.

"Farleigh," she told him. "But I been living in New York for a while."

"Figures. You talk like city. Fillin' in for them Toms who works for 'em in town, hunh?"

Blanche nodded. "What about you?"

"I been working for this family since Miz Em was a girl. Come here to work when I was twelve years old. So was Miz Em. We got the same birthday, ya know." Nate hooked his thumbs in the straps of his overalls. "I worked for her daddy and her daddy's daddy. Outlived both them suckers." Nate chortled a vicious little laugh and headed for the back door. "I was looking forward to going to Miz Em's funeral, too," he added. "But now…"

"Why you say that? She ain't dead yet, and neither are you."

Nate hesitated. "Miz Grace is one of them kinda people always worried about her standin' in the community—that's how she puts it, like she was some kinda church or the government or something. That's how I know it's got to be him that's behind this mess."

"What mess? You mean the new will?"

Nate went on talking, but he didn't answer Blanche's questions. "I never thought he was much. Course, he thinks plenty of hisself. Hardest work the man does is brushin' back his hair. Unless you call gamblin' and runnin' after women 'work.' He's kinda like a pet Miz Grace bought to show off to her friends. To prove she could get her a man, too, I guess, even though he *is* a hand-me-down, so to speak." Nate rubbed his jaw. His whiskers rasping against his hand sounded like shifting sand.

"Maybe I made a mistake," he said. "Maybe I was wrong 'bout him bein' too lazy to cause any harm 'cept to run through Miz Grace's money quick fast and in a hurry. Or so they say."

"I still don't understand," Blanche told him.

Nate opened the back door, then turned to look at her. His eyes called her to attention. "You don't need to understand," he told her. "I wisht I didn't." He put on his baseball cap. "You look after yourself, Miz City." He tipped his cap in her direction and went quickly out the door.

Blanche followed him and called softly to him to come back. Nate waved to her over his shoulder, shook his head from side to side, and kept on going. Blanche could tell from the way he shook his head that it was useless to run after him. He was through talking to her for the night. Tears of disappointment sprang to her eyes. She hadn't realized how tightly she'd latched on to him, the only black person she'd been with since she'd left home for the courthouse. Once she'd gotten a glimpse of who he really was, she wanted to ask him how it was that Mumsfield didn't know about Emmeline's alcoholism, what it was that made Grace so nervous, and why had he changed into a statue in Emmeline's room. But he was gone, and she was standing there being a meal for the mosquitoes. She swatted at one buzzing near her ear.

The night wrapped itself lovingly around her limbs. Some long-locked door creaked open almost wide enough for her to see inside, to remember how it was she knew the night so well and felt so very comfortable in it. With her moment of near-remembrance came a sense of personal worth, of strength, and fearlessness that buoyed her. She was distracted from her memory by a sharp bite on her ankle. But the feeling roused by her almost-recollection was so sweet she couldn't let it go. She turned out the kitchen light and sat down on the back stoop.

The stars were bright and silver-blue. The moon was a child's drawing, lopsided, bright, and full of magic. Blanche stretched out her arms and let her head fall back. She could feel muscles pulling in her forearms and tightening at the back of her neck. She relaxed against the step and stared out into the deeper dark that hung above the garden and in the pinewoods beyond.

Night Girl. She hadn't thought about her private game for years.

Cousin Murphy was responsible for Blanche's becoming Night Girl, when Cousin Murphy found eight-year-old Blanche crying because some kids had teased her about being so black.

"Course they tease you!" Cousin Murphy had told Blanche. She'd leaned over the crouching child as she spoke. Blanche could still smell her Midnight Blue perfume and see her breasts hanging long and lean from her tall, thin frame.

"Them kids is just as jealous of you as they can be! That's why they tease you," Cousin Murphy had told her. "They jealous 'cause you got the night in you. Some people got night in 'em, some got morning, others, like me and your mama, got dusk. But it's only them that's got night can become invisible. People what got night in 'em can step into the dark and poof—disappear! Go any old where they want. Do anything. Ride them stars up there, like as not. Shoot, girl, no wonder them kids teasing you. I'm a grown woman and I'm jealous, too!"

Cousin Murphy's explanation hadn't stopped kids from calling her Ink Spot and Tar Baby. But Cousin Murphy and Night Girl gave Blanche a sense of herself as special, as wondrous, and as powerful, all because of the part of her so many people despised, a part of her that she'd always known was directly connected to the heart of who she was.

It was then that she'd become Night Girl, slipping out of the house late at night to roam around her neighborhood unseen. She'd sometimes stop beside an overgrown azalea by a rickety front porch and learn from deep, earnest voices of neighborhood deaths and fights, wages gambled away, about-to-be-imprisoned sons and pregnant daughters, before her mother and her talkative friends had gotten the news. This prior knowledge had convinced Blanche's mother that her child had second sight.

Everything I was then, I am today. Blanche examined the idea and discovered all of her Night Girl courage and daring still in the safe in the back of her brain and growing more valuable every day. Without even realizing it, she drew on it when she needed to, like at the courthouse. Her break from there might turn out to have been a crazy thing to do, or it might not. In either case, it was the act of a take-charge kind of woman. A Night Girl kind of woman. Too bad she didn't also have the second sight her mother claimed for her. She could use it to make some sense of what Nate had said. She couldn't dismiss it. A black man in America couldn't live to get that old by being a fool. Tomorrow. She'd tackle him then. She yawned, said goodnight to the night, and went up to bed.

She lay naked on top of the sheets, hoping to attract a bit of the breeze she could hear stirring the pine trees. Despite the coolness of the evening, her high, narrow room was still full of afternoon warmth. She wondered if Taifa and Malik were asleep. She could see their round, plump faces, replicas of their daddy's sloe-eyed Geechee good looks. Did they suspect something was wrong? Kids were so good at feeling out situations.

She fell into a fitful sleep in which she was chasing a blood-red bus down a long, narrow highway and was in turn being chased by Mumsfield. Trees with prison matron branches reached out for her, but she knew she'd be safe as long as she kept moving.

"What do you think, Blanche? I trust you, Blanche!" Mumsfield shouted from behind. But she couldn't spare the breath to respond.

Up ahead, Malik and Taifa beckoned frantically from the back of the bus. She was carrying Mumsfield's automobile tools under her left arm. Instead of her own hair, big, fat gray sausage curls flopped about on her head.

FOUR

n the morning, Blanche put on underwear still slightly damp from last night's washing. While she sipped her first cup of tea at the kitchen table, she listened for voices, footsteps, or the sound of water running overhead. Nothing. Ordinarily, she'd have flipped on the radio and twiddled the dial until she found something other than hillbilly music and preaching. Radio—especially late-night radio, when she could pick up stations from California and French-speaking stations from Quebec—soothed and energized her. It provided living proof that the world was still out there and, therefore, at least theoretically within her grasp. The most nasal and nagging of her employers' voices could be tuned out if the radio was playing. She'd once been a TV soaps addict. But there were too many people on it telling her she needed to look and act and buy like them in order to be all right. Radio was willing to go where she went and to let her decide what the people whose voices she heard looked like. But this morning her plans required quiet.

Grace had told her they'd want breakfast at 8:30. The kitchen clock said 6:15. A good time to pay a visit to the front rooms. Blanche regularly used the front rooms in houses where she worked for more than a day. It was something she had to do, it would be bad luck not to. She preferred to wait until her employers were out and were expected to be gone for some time. But, to her knowledge, these people had no plans to go anywhere, and she would be in the house only a few more days. She had to take her chance while she could. Twice she'd been caught taking liberties with her employers' space. Both times she'd been in the bathtub.

The first time she'd been caught by Hazel Spence, a rich Long Island widow for whom she'd worked two days a week for nearly two years. The widow had called Blanche's use of her bathtub, bath salts, inflatable bath pillow, and elegant back brush a breach of her privacy, if not an illegal use of her possessions. She'd fired Blanche on the spot and refused to pay her the wages she'd already earned.

The second time she'd been caught by David Lee Palmer, the brother of her first Farleigh customer. He'd made her pay in a much more painful and private way. She hadn't bothered to report it to the police. Even if they'd believed her and cared about the rape of a black woman by a white man, once it came out that she'd been attacked while naked in her employer's bathtub, she'd never have been employed in anybody's house in town again. But she still had hopes of fixing that motherless piece of shit one day.

Neither incident had stopped her from taking her ease among the items she spent her time tending. On the few occasions that she'd stopped to think about what she was doing, she'd recognized that sitting in their chairs, looking out their windows, using their telephones and stereos were ways of getting some of her sold self back. For while the work beat anything else she'd tried—it at least didn't have the routine of an assembly line or the tyranny of a supervisor out to make promotion—she wouldn't be doing it if she didn't need the money. If she had money, she'd move to the Caribbean and open a guesthouse for hardworking women like herself: reasonably priced comfort, good food, no men or children allowed.

Now she walked slowly down the hall toward the living room, once again listening for sounds or movement from above. Still nothing. If no one had been at home, she might have switched on the stereo. There was a time when she'd have gone to the television and turned on a soap opera. But she'd given up soaps when she'd found herself worrying about whether Meg should marry Peter or Carl on *Moments of Our Lives* on the very same day that she lost her wallet, got a notice from her landlord saying her building was being condoed out of her price range, and one of her best-paying clients announced she was moving to Europe. She'd decided then that she didn't need to be involved with anything that kept her from dealing with the real world, since it was surely going to deal with her, no matter who Meg married. Nowadays, she was more likely to loll in an easy chair and leaf through whatever books or magazines might be about. Over the years, she'd picked up information on everything from medicine to map-making from her employers' reading material.

She fluffed a few cushions and wiped a speck of dust from the coffee table before choosing her seat. She sat on the sofa. The chair where Grace had sat crying provided a better view, but Blanche didn't go near it. Gloom and tension still hung around that chair. She leaned her head back against the comfortable sofa and put her foot up on the edge of the coffee table. She let her eyes roam over the scene out the window. It was another lovely Carolina morning. The pine trees were blue-green in the morning sun. She could hear three different birds' songs, none of which she could identify. In between the chirping and whistling and twittering was the sound of the pine trees rustling like women switching in silk petticoats. Blanche set her mind to rest there, on the view, thinking of nothing, only seeing and listening, marveling. She was always amazed at how very beautiful the everyday world was down here after the concrete bleakness of most of New York.

Despite her crazy dream, she had slept well and had risen with more optimism than she'd felt since she took off from the courthouse. She had a plan. With a little luck, she was just hours, at the most days, away from getting her tax return. Ardell was to pick up the check, borrow Leo's car, meet Blanche, and take her someplace where she could cash it. She'd ask Ardell to bring the kids to meet her, so they could talk about her leaving and say their goodbyes. After that, she and Ardell would drive to Durham, where Blanche would get the bus north. She saw herself as already gone from this place, from this state, out of the sheriff's reach. It wouldn't take her more than a year to get herself enough steady customers or a long-term position with a decent wage. She was very good at and proud of what she did in a world where that combination was harder to find in many professions. Somehow she would convince her mother to give up the children when she was settled. Just as she would find a way to make the children understand that her leaving them behind was both necessary and temporary. They had surely built enough trust in her by now for them to handle it—which was not to say that any of it was going to be easy on anybody.

At the same time, Blanche caught her breath at the thought of months without kids to tend, of once again taking whatever risks she saw fit with no concern for anything beyond herself, as long as she could send money to her mother. There's nothing wrong with looking forward to having my own life back for a little while, she defended herself. After all, she hadn't chosen to be a mother. She scoffed at the inner voice which argued that she could have refused her sister's request. How did you say no to your dying, widowed sister? When Rosalie had asked her to take the children, the cancer had already spread beyond her breasts. Blanche had agreed, almost in the belief that by doing so she was warding off the inevitability of Rosalie's death. Rosalie's other legacy was the unanswered and unanswerable question of whether Rosalie had meant to punish her by making her the children's guardian.

Blanche had never made a secret of her decision not to have children. Rosalie had always chided Blanche about it, calling her selfish and unwomanly. It didn't bother Blanche. She understood her sister too well. But it bothered Rosalie. Rosalie had never been able to accept that her way of life wasn't the preferred way for everyone she cared about. For over a year after her death, Blanche had hated her dead sister for having proscribed her life.

But she knew that Rosalie had loved her children dearly. She would never have left them to someone she didn't believe would really care for them and love them, no matter what her other motives might have been. And I'm sure as hell hooked now! she laughed to herself and shook her head. She sat for a few more minutes, then rose, adjusted the crotch of her panties, and went to the front door.

She'd heard a car in the drive around five that morning and assumed it was someone delivering the newspaper. Evidence of the soundness of her hearing and assumption lay on the stoop. Her heart skipped twice as she leaned down to pick it up. There would be no picture of her, she was sure of that, only her name. Enough to make her mother and her children both frightened and ashamed, not to mention how the people in this house would react. She turned the newspaper in her hands, stared at the ducks gliding across the pond, and tried to quiet her breathing. The newspaper rustled. She willed her hands to stop shaking, took the paper back to the sofa, and scanned the front page. Nothing. Nothing inside the paper either. She knew her crime was a piddling bit of business compared to murder or robbery. It hadn't even occurred to her that her escape would make the regional radio and TV news. She was glad her mother and children would be spared reading about her in the newspaper. But she'd expected a certain amount of local fuss. She'd outfoxed her so-called betters, tricked those who needed very badly to believe she was too dumb to do so. The sheriff's office wouldn't take kindly to it. So, there was something frightening about this lack of mention in the paper. She searched its pages once again, article by article. Still nothing. She was about to have one last look, when the hair on the back of her neck rose to attention. She changed her position from sitting on the sofa to leaning over it, plumping up the cushions.

"Good morning, sir."

"Why, good morning, Blanche White!" There was a chuckle in Everett's voice. He drew her name out so that it sounded like a taunt. "You're looking quite chipper this morning. Country air seems to agree with you."

"Yes, sir, I always did like the country." Despite the company, she added to herself.

"Well, I'm sure we're delighted to have you, Blanche White."

There it was again. Blanche checked his eyes for malice but found only laughter of the teasing variety.

"You ain't mocking me, are you, sir?"

His eyes widened slightly. "Sensitive, aren't we?"

"Isn't that what you hoped...sir?"

She braced herself for his pulling rank and putting her in her so-called place. Instead, a hint of red crept up from his neck. He brushed back his already perfect hair and managed a contrite smile. He didn't apologize, of course. That was far too much to expect from a pretty boy who'd probably been admonished only twice in his life, and never by the likes of her. She held the newspaper out to him.

"Thank you, Blanche." This time there was no joking about her name.

Blanche went back to the kitchen and turned on the radio, but she paid little attention to the sounds that trickled into the room. Her mind was still on Everett. She'd expected him to challenge her, to pretend he'd done nothing wrong and claim that she was out of line. Actually, he'd come as close to admitting he'd been wrong as a man like him probably could. She sifted flour and baking powder into a bowl. Maybe he wasn't as full of himself as his preening as Nate made him seem. Of course, he was always on his good behavior with Grace. It's her aunt that's got the money, she mumbled aloud. She turned to the door as she spoke. Mumsfield was already smiling when he opened the door.

"Did you say something, Blanche?"

"Good morning, Mumsfield, honey. Don't mind me. I'm just talking to myself." She added milk and eggs to the flour, along with a pinch of sugar, and stirred.

"I talk to myself to keep from having to talk to fools!" Mumsfield said in a shaky but sharp old-lady voice.

Blanche gave him a questioning look.

"That's what Aunt Em says," he giggled.

Blanche nodded, impressed with his ability to change his voice. Even though he didn't sound like Emmeline, he did sound like an elderly woman. Blanche added three tablespoons of melted butter to the pancake batter and resumed stirring.

"After breakfast, we go to town, Blanche. I drive." He puffed out his chest a bit when he delivered his "I drive" line. He had on his yellow suspenders again.

"We who, Mumsfield, honey?"

"Us, Blanche. You and me. Now I go to buy gas." He gave her his scrunched-together smile and bounced out the back door.

Grace repeated Mumsfield's information about the trip to town when she came to the kitchen to fetch Emmeline's breakfast tray.

"Dr. Haley is expecting you." Grace laced and unlaced her fingers. "He says he has a tonic that may help Aunt Emmeline." She gave Blanche a meaning-laden look. Blanche wondered just what kind of tonic. There was no bottled cure for alcoholism, as far as she knew. It was probably something to help the old girl sleep off her gin jones. Or maybe Grace and Everett just want Mumsfield and me out of the way so they can romp through the house in the nude. It made an amusing mental picture, if not a very likely one.

Grace continued to stand silently chafing her hands and blinking like a broken stoplight. Either Emmeline or that husband of hers is driving this girl's blood pressure right on up there! Blanche thought.

"Mumsfield knows the way to Dr. Haley's office." Grace bared her teeth in forced cheeriness that only made her anxiety more apparent.

"You all right, ma'am?"

"Oh…I…Yes, I'm fine. She…Oh, Blanche, she's just so cruel when she's like this…So cruel and…" She shook her head and fell silent.

After her encounter with Emmeline, Blanche knew exactly what Grace meant, which was why Blanche wasn't about to volunteer to take Emmeline's tray up again. She was tempted to suggest the Aunt Daisy solution, but it occurred to her that someone was already supplying Emmeline, which meant the meal ticket's wishes were not to be messed with.

Grace shook her head as though to clear it. "Mumsfield could fetch the tonic himself, but we always feel better when someone rides with him. Oh, he's an excellent driver. He's never had an accident or even a parking ticket. But you see how he is. On his own, he's liable to roam into a mechanic's shop somewhere and forget to come home until nightfall!" A mirthless grin punctuated her words.

Blanche decided to take advantage of Grace's explaining mood. "Excuse me for asking, ma'am, but just what is his condition?"

Grace's eyes widened. Her intake of breath was quite audible, but, as Blanche had hoped, the surprise of being asked prompted an response.

"Mosaicism," Grace said. "A kind of Down's syndrome but not as bad. He's been to a special school and can read and write, and, of course, drive. And he's quite smart in some ways. Cars, and…" Grace's training finally overrode her shock. She stopped speaking and simply stared at Blanche in disbelief. It was all right for the "madam" to tell her "girl" the most intimate family details, but it was not all right for the girl to bluntly ask. They both knew that, her look seemed to say.

Grace picked up Emmeline's tray. "You may leave a cold lunch for my husband and me…and Aunt, of course." Ice crystals formed on the tips of Grace's words. She pulled herself up to her full height, picking up any bit of I'm-the-boss she might have dropped by answering Blanche's question. If she had any concern for when Mumsfield and Blanche might have lunch, or what they might eat, she didn't voice it.

"And don't forget to go home and get your uniforms and things for the rest of the week." Grace had already turned on her heel and was heading for the door to the dining room.

"And I can stop by the agency and get things straightened out," Blanche suggested. She was so pleased with herself for having found a way to put the agency problem to rest, at least in Grace's mind, that she didn't even mind Grace's lack of response.

An hour or so later, she was in the car beside Mumsfield, squeezed between Blanche's fear of being picked up by the police the minute she set foot in Farleigh and the hope of talking to Taifa and Malik. She knew the urge to talk to them was heightened by her decision to leave them with her mother for a while. Maybe it was unfair, but she wanted to hear them loving her on the phone once more before they learned she was leaving and pain and anger crept into their voices.

Mumsfield was quiet as they left the secondary road for the highway. He still hadn't said a word by the time they reached the entrance to the highway. It was as though he and the car and the road were joined in a sacred pact that forbade him from paying attention to anything else. This is one of the ways he's different, Blanche thought. It's like he can almost become the thing he's doing. Everything else is off to the side, at the corner of his eye. I could use some of that. Of course, she could use anything that made her feel less like a Ping-Pong ball in a hurricane, despite her plans. She cleared her mind and focused on the green hills in the distance and the extra-blue sky. She let her shoulders drop and felt some of the tension seep out of her neck. The world is still beautiful, she told herself, and I'm still in it. Everything else can be put right, in time.

Dr. Haley lived in a large white house down a narrow driveway lined with forsythia. When she rang the bell, he answered the door himself and handed her a mid-sized bottle neatly wrapped in brown paper. He waved to Mumsfield and watched as he turned the car around and headed back down the drive.

Blanche directed Mumsfield to the parking lot behind Meg's Diner, at the corner of Main and Centre Streets. She told him she had a few errands to run and left him in the diner with two cheeseburgers, a double order of French fries, cole slaw, a chocolate shake, and the promise that she'd meet him at that very spot in an hour and a half. She was nearly out the door, around the corner, and in the phone booth by the time Mumsfield said goodbye to her.

She heaved a sigh as she dialed the phone and tried to make herself ready for the wave of questioning and scolding she knew was about to crash over her. "Mama?" she said when the phone was answered on the other end, then quickly held the receiver away from her ear.

"Blanche! Where the devil are you? I can't stand this...My pressure...You give me that phone number so I can...And one of them nasty sheriff's deputies been here, asking a bunch of tomfool questions. I told him what you said, 'bout New Orleans, Lord forgive me. I don't like lyin', it ain't right! The Lord said..."

Despite her mother's screeching and preaching, Blanche had to smile. It was good to know Mama was still there, still herself, still all right. When the volume and speed of her mother's tirade had lessened a little, Blanche decided it was her turn to talk. "Mama!" She spoke just loud enough to be heard over her mother's voice. "I'm gonna hang up this phone if you say one more word before I get a chance to tell you what I got to say!"

Her mother stopped talking so abruptly that for a moment Blanche was herself struck dumb. It was rare that Miz Cora did as she was told. Blanche took a deep breath and launched into the story of all that had happened to her since she'd walked the kids to her mother's, kissed them goodbye, told them to be good, and headed downtown to the courthouse.

When she'd finished, Blanche was surprised that her mother didn't urge her to turn herself in. That was the sort of advice she

expected from the let-us-love-one-another brand of Christianity
her mother professed. But Miz Cora didn't urge her to seek God's
guidance or to serve Jesus through humility.

"What about your cousin Charlotte, up there in Boston?
Every Christmas she sends me a card thanking me for taking in
that boy of hers when he got in that trouble with the police up
there. I didn't want to be bothered with that big ole hulking boy at
the time, but you…Anyways, why don't I call her on the telephone
and tell her to expect you? Better'n that New York, seems to me…
And I'll send the kids on up just as soon as you say…this time."

It was as though her mother had suddenly stepped outside
of that turn-the-other-cheek fantasy land she and so many other
older black people Blanche knew seemed to live in. But then, why
should I be surprised? she asked herself. This is how we've sur-
vived in this country all this time, by knowing when to act like
we believe what we've been told and when to act like we know
what we know.

"Yes, Mama, I'll get out of the state as soon as I can lay hands
on my income-tax check. It should be there by the time these
people come back to town next week…I'm glad it wasn't in the
paper either, although it seems kinda odd."

"Maybe the sheriff's office ain't ready for no more bad publicity," her mother told her. "They investigatin' his office, you
know. And just last week, a drunken deputy broke his leg leaving
that cathouse down the end of Cressfield Street. That wasn't in
the paper either."

Blanche hadn't known that her mother was so knowledgeable about that end of Cressfield Street and what went on there.
"No, Mama, I'm not being nosy about these people's business.
I only know what Mumsfield—yes, he's the boy—only what he
told me. I didn't ask him anything, much," Blanche said. "Yes, I
know it's dangerous, but…All right, Mama, all right…and thank
you, Mama, for everything. Now, please let me talk to Taifa and
Malik."

It hadn't even occurred to Blanche that the kids might not be around. Her disappointment was made worse when her mother reminded her this was the Saturday Leo had promised to take them fishing. All the loving reassurance she'd planned to push through the phone now lay in her stomach like stone soup. "You didn't tell him anything, did you, Mama?"

"Course I told him something! You think I want that man runnin' round here acting like a lovesick fool? I told him you was workin' in the country this week. At least that ain't a lie. I done told enough of them for you, girl! I swear you gon' make me lose my place in heaven!"

"Thanks, Mama. I'll call you again when I can." Blanche cut her mother off before she got up another full head of steam. "Tell the kids I love them and whatever else you think you should." Blanche broke the connection but continued to grip the receiver. She turned her face to the phone-booth wall and cried her longing to hear her children's voices into the dead receiver. Self-preservation finally propelled her out of the phone booth.

She stuffed her soggy handkerchief in her handbag and walked four blocks to the downtown shopping district. Her first stop was the Salvation Army secondhand store on Sixth Street, where she bought a pink and white seersucker bathrobe. She walked two blocks east, past the courthouse and the Civil War monument (at which she slyly spit, as was her habit), and a block south to Woolworth's. Here she bought two pairs of rubber gloves. She never trusted employers to supply them and she couldn't work without them. Along with the gloves, she bought a set of underwear, including two pairs of queen-sized pantyhose. As usual, the latter purchase made her think that if she were a queen, she sure as hell wouldn't stuff herself into a pair of sausage casings. She also bought a toothbrush, a cake of Ivory soap, and a folding suitcase on sale for three-ninety-nine. When she was through shopping, she had fifty-seven dollars and seventy-two cents, enough to last a couple of weeks, or a month or so, if

Cousin Charlotte could provide room and board until she found work.

The urge to leave now made the bottoms of her feet itch. She was just three blocks from the Trailways station. Her income-tax check seemed far away and unreal compared to the solid rectangle of the bus station. She could take the bus over to Durham and wait there for her check. Her friend Margie would put her up for a few nights, until Ardell could get her check for her. Blanche could feel the bus rolling along beneath her, see the trees and fields hurrying by as she moved farther and farther away from Farleigh. Oh, Grace would be in a snit and call up the agency, but wouldn't the agency cover for her to save their own ass? After all, they hadn't owned up to not knowing who the hell she was, for fear of offending the Mistress of the Manor. They'd think of some story in order to keep Grace's business and good will. And was it really likely that either Grace or the agency would call the sheriff? She'd just be living up to their view of all black people as irresponsible. She turned left and walked toward the station. A big interstate bus passed her, heading out of town. She quickened her pace. As the station came into sight, she suddenly saw Mumsfield sitting patiently back at the diner waiting for her for hours, trusting that she'd come back because she'd said she would.

Damn! I didn't ask that boy to trust me! He'd done her a favor by not telling his cousins that she hadn't worked for them before, but that didn't make them friends. A friend would have told him the real reason he was being kept from his aunt, especially since he was blaming himself for Emmeline's illness. A friend would tell him his cousins might have plans to mess with his money. If they were friends, she would be able to tell him about her troubles and ask for his help in getting away. The idea was ridiculous. He was rich and white, and his handicap excluded him from much of what went on in his own world. It certainly minimized what little ability he might have had to understand her life, especially her present situation. She was sure he looked on the sheriff, or any law enforcement officer, as a friend. He might even ask that kind-hearted waitress at the diner to call the sheriff because his friend Blanche was missing. She wondered if anybody was working on a vaccine against Darkies' Disease. She hurried into the station and stood in one of the ticket lines. Her legs had that "Run!" feeling again. She looked around the station to distract herself from the shouting in her head that said she should stop and think for a second. She was reminded of her last minutes in the courtroom, when she'd longed for someone to look at her, pay attention to what was being done to her. No one looked at anyone else here, either. But something happened that got everyone's attention.

She heard the siren just before the sheriff's car made a sharp, fast turn off the street, bounced over the curb into the bus station parking lot, and came to a screeching halt. Blanche quickly sidestepped out of line and out the side exit to her left. She hurried across the street against the light and walked back the way she had come.

"I like your suspenders," she told Mumsfield when they were once again in the limousine.

He nodded his head slowly a few times, in a way that gave the subject of suspenders more weight than Blanche had ever suspected it had. "Suspenders are very important, Blanche."

"Colors, too," she added.

"Oh, yes! Yellow suspenders make driving the best. Safe."

"Umm hmm." It was Blanche's turn to nod in agreement. "And red for fixing cars, and orange for eating."

"Yes, Blanche! You understand, Blanche!" He obviously thought she was quite clever to do so. Blanche chuckled to herself. This boy had more parts than a picture puzzle.

On the way to the country house, she asked Mumsfield if he'd mind some music and was lucky enough to find a radio station playing Diana Ross. She felt better with Diana in the car. Diana's voice was like a ribbon tying Blanche to the part of the world she knew and needed. It wasn't simply her singing that soothed Blanche. Diana had once been poor, just like Blanche. If Diana could move from the welfare and the housing projects of Detroit to the top of the music charts and starring roles in movies, certainly Blanche could get herself out of this mess she was in, just as black women had been getting themselves and their people out of messes in this country since the day the first kidnapped African woman was dragged onto these shores. And wasn't she Night Girl, too? She saw herself holding Taifa and Malik's hands while the three of them looked up at the memorial to black Civil War soldiers that she'd once read was somewhere in downtown Boston. She leaned her head back against the seat and a smile curved her lips. In a little while, her eyelids drooped, her breathing slowed. It was the stopping of the car in the driveway of the country house that waked her. She emerged from a dream about taking the kids to an amusement park into the nightmare of the sheriff's car parked in front of the house.

FIVE

Just as when she'd been sentenced, Blanche's bowels reacted to the sight of the sheriff's car. But this time there was no ladies' room for her to hurry into and from which to escape. For a few moments she sat in the limousine, trying to get control of her sphincter muscles and staring out into the perfect summer day. Her eyes devoured grass and flowers, the height of the pines, the way the mockingbird on the lawn bobbed its tail. She took it all in as if to fortify herself with leaf green and sky blue before the man talking to Everett locked her away someplace gray and cruel.

The sheriff raised his hand, his palm toward Everett's chest, not touching him and not meaning to. Everett swayed back on his heels as though nearly pushed off balance by the force of the sheriff's gesture.

"Are you all right, Blanche?" Mumsfield leaned over and touched her arm. "You look funny, Blanche."

Blanche shook her head and opened the car door. She forced her feet to move toward the house. How did he find me? she wondered. Her legs twitched with the longing to run as fast as possible in the opposite direction. She clenched her teeth and cautioned herself not to cry or show fear.

The sheriff swung away from Everett and stepped in front of her. He reached out and tapped her on the arm. She managed not to flinch.

"Don't I know you, gal?" He moved closer to her, peering up into her face with squinty brown eyes. His little girl's voice some-how made the question seem more ominous.

Why was he toying with her? So he could reveal her as a liar as well as an escaped prisoner? She knew she must answer his question but wasn't sure she could stop herself from begging him to please have mercy on her, to at least let her see her children before she was dragged off to jail. She cleared her throat and wondered if he could smell the fear rising from her in acrid, sweaty waves. Would she be less scared now if this shrimpy, pot-bellied man were less well known for abusing black and poor people? Some folks thought it was being not much bigger and heavier than his tin badge that made him so mean. Blanche thought it was his genes.

"I said," the sheriff repeated, "don't I know you, gal?" His stringy hair quivered as he spoke. His breath smelled of bile. For a second, her concern about being imprisoned was superseded by the possibility that the spittle glistening in the corners of his mouth might suddenly fly up into her face. She could already feel it, cold and acid against her cheek.

"Oh, yes, sir," she finally managed to say. She wondered whose high, squeaky voice was coming out of her mouth. "Sometimes I help out in the kitchen at the Pettigrew place." She literally held her breath. If he wasn't playing games with her, would he believe her? All the domestic help in town knew the sheriff regularly delivered the very drunk Miss Hazeline Pettigrew Conroy, heiress to the Pettigrew fortune, into the arms of one or another servant at the back door of the Pettigrew plantation. Just as everyone knew that old man Pettigrew had gotten the sheriff his job.

The sheriff didn't bother to respond. He simply turned from her to Everett, dismissing her with his lack of interest. Blanche let her breath out in a rush and hurried inside to the bathroom.

Relief made her light-headed. She fought the urge to laugh hard and long. Twice now she'd managed to use her wits to save herself. The old folks said things happened in threes. Did that mean she was going to have to rescue herself once again before she could get away clean?

She soaped and washed her hands and the place on her arm where Sheriff Stillwell had touched her. She fought the urge to actively wish him ill. Those kinds of wishes often seemed to boomerang. And it wasn't necessary to wish the sheriff ill. All she had to hope for was that life provided him with exactly what he deserved. She looked into the medicine cabinet mirror, almost expecting to see an unfamiliar face, as though her ability to fool the sheriff had been aided by a newfound ability to alter her looks and turn herself into someone else. No one, not even the sheriff, was likely to look for her here in this house. Unreleased laughter coursed through her, freshening her blood, restoring the sheen to her skin that her scare with the sheriff had erased. Now, if her income-tax check would only come.

She hummed a bit off-key while she loaded the dishwasher with lunch dishes, then wheeled the vacuum cleaner into the front of the house. Everett was nowhere in sight and neither was Grace. Out the front window, she could see Mumsfield shining the hood of the limousine. The sheriff's car was gone.

She quickly ran the vacuum cleaner over the living room floor. But why was the sheriff here if he wasn't looking for her? Blanche's movements slowed as her vision turned inward. She could see the sheriff holding up his hand, like a traffic cop, as though Everett's words were a line of cars to be halted. When the sheriff had turned away from Everett to hassle her, he hadn't even bothered to excuse himself to Everett. She thought the sheriff had stopped her only to show Everett he was the man in charge, even of the people in Everett's employ. Everett had been so stiff he was almost trembling. Why? At the time, she'd thought Everett was outraged by Stillwell's uppityness. Now she wasn't so sure. Could it have been fear that had nearly knocked Everett off his feet? She'd been so frightened herself it hadn't occurred to her that there was any fear left for anyone else. She recalled a kind of trapped animal look on Everett's face. But what did the sheriff have to say that would frighten Everett? She shook her head and stepped up the pace of her vacuuming. If I need to know, I'll find out, she told herself with a certainty born of her victory over the sheriff.

She lugged the vacuum and a bucket holding a feather duster, furniture polish, chamois, sponge, spray cleaner, and a long-handled brush up the back stairs. She had no intention of using all of these items, but it looked good to have them. She dropped the lot at the top of the stairs and looked at the seven doors ranging on either side of the hall. She knew the far door on the right belonged to Emmeline. She didn't feel like dealing with a drunk at the moment, so she knocked on the door closest to her and on the opposite side of the hall from Emmeline's room. No answer. She opened the door to find a built-in linen closet full of sets of sheets, hand towels, and blankets in zippered plastic bags. Beyond the closet, the rest of the room was full of boxes with labels like Living Room Dust Covers, Shutters, and Croquet Set. The room next to the storage room was a bathroom with no towels and the fusty air of disuse.

The smell of machine oil and chocolate greeted her when she eased open the first door on the right-hand side of the corridor. Mumsfield's room: silver foil candy wrappers on the floor by the bed, a model car on the night table, pictures of cars and clocks on the walls. An oily machine part lay on newspaper on a table by the door that led to the bathroom. The machine part reminded her of men gathered in garages, oiling cars, talking about women, and sipping beer, not an image she associated with Mumsfield. Why had she expected a train set and marbles? She guessed Mumsfield to be about twenty-five. Maybe it had as much to do with what she heard and saw as what she felt, like the way Everett talked to him and Grace talked about him. Even though he was allowed to drive the car and could probably take it apart and put it together again, he wasn't to be taken seriously as a person. Something they shared.

She went back into the hall to fetch her cleaning supplies and met Grace, who gave her a tight little smile but said nothing. She passed Blanche, knocked on the door of Emmeline's room, spoke her own name as if in response to Emmeline's question, although Blanche didn't hear the question, then entered the room. Blanche returned to Mumsfield's room and gave it a quick dust and shine.

The room next to Mumsfield's belonged to Everett. Blanche realized it was possible and logical for the room to belong to both Grace and Everett, but she didn't think so. It smelled like a man's room, no hint of that light, flowery scent Grace wore, only something sharp and heavy that she could identify only as a man-smell. And there was nothing of Grace to be seen, no slippers, no nightgown at the foot of the bed. There was plenty of Everett around. His bureau was littered with change, keys, a sock. A pair of shorts were thrown over the arm of the chair by the window. The sheets and light blanket were tangled into a knot that sat in the middle of the bed like a cherry on a sundae. His bathroom was a heap of damp towels.

She might have taken such sloppiness to signify someone who was too busy, too miserable, too hurried or distracted to give time or thought to neatness. None of those conditions applied to Everett as far as she could see. He didn't appear to be working at any job other than preening himself and humoring Grace. Blanche had seen him both angry and agitated, but he seemed neither unhappy or harried. She pulled on a pair of the rubber gloves she'd bought in town before gathering up Everett's stray clothes. If she were planning to take these folks on as regular customers, she'd tell him about leaving his dirty underwear lying about. She didn't consider picking up people's funky drawers from the floor a normal part of her work. She expected her employers to put their soiled underwear in the hamper and their soiled tissues in the wastebasket. She considered this behavior as a sign of what her mother called "couth," and a good indicator of whether or not she could expect any respect from a customer— and whether she'd be with that customer for very long.

She pictured herself holding his smelly socks under his nose until he understood that she had some rights, too. But he'd probably pass out first! she laughed to herself. She knew she might be exaggerating Everett's arrogance, but she wasn't exaggerating the way he'd smirked in her face then teased her about her name, or the ignorant way he shouted when he talked to Mumsfield, as though trying to penetrate an extra-thick skull with his voice. He also wasn't too tolerant of people who crossed him, if his angry comment about Emmeline was any evidence. Still, he hadn't exactly jumped with both feet into the sheriff's chest. It all added up to a contradiction. "Just like everybody else," she mumbled to herself.

She put Everett's room in order and shut his door firmly behind her. She moved down the hall, past the main staircase. She was unconsciously humming the usual flat tune of her own composition. She knocked at the door to the left of Emmeline's room—a guest room draped in sheets. As she closed the door and stepped back into the hall, she noticed that Emmeline's door was not completely shut. She heard Emmeline's voice hit a high, complaining note, followed by a measured mumble from Grace. Blanche stood still and listened.

"Get out, you two-faced bitch," Emmeline screeched at the top of her lungs. Blanche jumped back, then took a few steps closer to Emmeline's door.

"I remember what they used to say about you! I'm watching you, don't you think I'm not, you sly cow!" Emmeline's voice was high and wild. Blanche couldn't make out Grace's reply.

When Grace came out of the room, Blanche had moved away and was dusting the small table near the top of the main stairs. At first, Grace seemed not to notice Blanche. She leaned against Emmeline's door and closed her eyes for a few seconds. When she opened them, they were moist. Her lips were a hard pink line. Big red spots, like clown makeup, dotted both her cheeks. She pushed herself away from the door and walked toward Blanche.

"Please don't disturb my aunt just now, Blanche," she said at last. "She's…resting. And the room next to hers is just a guest room, so you needn't bother with it, either," she added.

Blanche watched Grace as she went down the stairs. She heard the front door close. She slipped back into Mumsfield's room and looked out the window. Grace was walking slowly toward the duck pond, her head thrown slightly back and her arms folded across her chest.

I should have done the old lady's room first, Blanche chided herself. Might've had a ringside seat for the shouting match. More likely it would have been postponed. Blanche stared at Emmeline's door for a few moments, bristling with the desire to knock and trying to conquer her natural inclination to defy the voice of authority. It was one of the reasons she had not lasted in the waitressing, telephone sales, clerking, and typing jobs she'd tried over the years. She always returned to domestic work. For all the *châtelaine* fantasies of some of the women for whom she worked, she was really her own boss, and her clients knew it. She was the expert. She ordered her employers' lives, not the other way around. She told them when they had to be out of the way, when she would work, and when she wouldn't. Or at least that's the way it was most of the time. Now she sighed in frustration and turned away from Emmeline's door.

She didn't bother to knock on the door on the right, next to Everett's room. It had to be Grace's room. She went in, and as if in reward for her decision to do as she was told, for a change, the room she entered was fascinating.

The white four-poster bed was hung with pale cotton drapes lined in white with tiny blue polka dots. The same cotton covered the seats of the two delicate-looking chairs and the table by the bed. It seemed a wonderfully calm place to hide, and Blanche congratulated Grace on being smart enough to provide it for herself. Yet, there was something about the room that made her uneasy. She looked around at the small items. These were the things most likely to tell her something about the person who occupied the room. Among these people, the furniture and pictures might have been chosen by a decorator.

What she noticed was that the old-fashioned silver-backed comb, brush, and hand-mirror set on top of the bureau looked exactly the same distance, one from the other. The top of the pen on the small desk across from the bed was lined up with the top of the leather writing paper case and the address book beside it. The clock on the bedside table was exactly the same distance from the water carafe as it was from the lamp. There was no radio, no television, not even a telephone to break the room's silence.

It seemed the wrong room for Grace. It was Everett, with his casually elegant clothes, fresh manicure, and well-shined shoes, from whom she'd have expected neatness. She'd once worked for a man who designed men's clothes and was himself known for his wardrobe and style. She'd picked up enough from him to know how much planning and study went into looking perfectly casual. But it was Grace, with the tail of her blouse peeking out from the top of her skirt and the edge of her slip from the bottom, who lived in this monument to unchanging order.

But despite the room's orderliness, its look of calm, the hair on Blanche's arms was stiff with electricity. The air felt nervous, jumpy. She walked around the room picking up the small clock, the hand mirror. She flicked the feather duster about as she went. The address book, with its floral-print cover, was also blue and white. GRACE CARTER HANCOCK was embossed at the top of the palest of blue stationery in the leather writing case. She was careful to replace each item in exactly the spot where she'd found it. She was aware of the time it took to get the items lined up properly and wondered if Grace was able to get them right the first time or if she, too, had to fiddle with them.

"Grace," she whispered, and the sound was full of questions about who this woman was. This was not the room of the Grace who knocked over her water glass and was nervous as a vampire at dawn. The Grace who kept this room like a shrine to herself was not the woman Everett hovered over maternally, or the one to whom Mumsfield made patient "Yes, Cousin" replies.

What is it about the people in this house and their rooms? Blanche asked herself. Except for Mumsfield, their rooms said one thing about who they were, and the way they looked and behaved said something else. Which was the true Everett—the well-groomed, caring, and gentle husband, or the arrogant slob who threw his funky socks on the dresser and was ready to attack the sheriff? And what about Emmeline? Was she just another drunk, or the sweet old lady Mumsfield talked about? Which Grace was real?

SIX

The next day, Blanche looked up from washing lettuce for lunch to see Everett and another man walking along the edge of the pinewoods surrounding the house. At first she didn't recognize the other man. She'd never before seen him without his boots, badge, and uniform, although she should have recognized those thin legs and the sad, droopy set of his belly. He looked even smaller without his gear, like any regular sawed-off, red-faced cracker, come hat in hand to curry favor from the gentry. Only the sheriff kept his hat on. If he'd been anyone else, she'd have cheered him on in his defiance of the class rules. Even without Stillwell's reputation and her present troubles, she didn't have much use for law enforcement people of any kind or color.

She still remembered the police beatings of people in the sixties, and the murders of young black and Puerto Rican males by cops in Harlem—at least one for every spring she'd lived in New York—as though they were deer in season. She'd watched the cops break down the apartment door of her neighbor Mrs. Castillo, beat the woman's husband unmercifully, and totally ransack their apartment, only to realize they had the wrong building. The policemen hadn't even apologized for the mess. In Blanche's mind, Southern law enforcement people were even worse: the descendants of the paddyrollers and overseers who'd made their living grinding her kind into fertilizer in the cotton fields of slavery.

As the two men walked, Everett sliced the air with his hands in a way that reminded Blanche of someone hacking through thick undergrowth with a machete.

"You in there, Miz City?" Nate called through the other kitchen window overlooking the backyard.

"Why's Stillwell hanging round here so much?" Blanche asked him, after their exchange of "How are you?" and "I'm fine," and after Blanche had poured him a glass of lemonade.

Nate eased himself onto a chair and watched Blanche over the rim of the glass with old onyx eyes. She sat in the chair across from him and poured herself a glass as well.

"Miz Grace used to spend her summers here, you know." Nate's eyes got the faraway look that goes with old memories. "Played right out there in that duck pond, she did. Paddling and splashing and shrieking at the top of her lungs. Wild as a polecat, she was."

Something in Nate's tone told her he had something particular to say. Nate rattled the ice in his glass. "Fact is, Miz Grace is kinda special to me, ya see." Uh oh. Blanche held her breath and hoped he wasn't about to destroy her growing respect for him with some Mr. Mammy bullshit.

"Back in 1959, when Miz Grace was about twelve years ole, things was real bad round here, real bad, even worse than they is today." Nate took a long swallow from his lemonade and took his time setting the glass back on the table. "White folks was bein' put off they land, and stores and shops was goin' bust, so you know how hard it was for us.

"Course, our bein' worse off didn't stop the gov'ment and all these low-life rednecks round here from blamin' us, like they always do. There was more Klan rallies going on round here, more talk 'bout protectin' the flower of Southern womanhood from thievin' black men, than you could shake a stick at! Naturally, all us colored kept to ourselves and kept as quiet as possible. Seems to me even the children played in a whisper."

Blanche heard Nate's voice as though it were coming from a distance, even though he sat just across the table from her. It was as though he'd slipped behind a thick glass wall where he was untouched by his own words and the thoughts that went with them. He sat perfectly still while he spoke.

"One night, round this time of year, a white woman's body was found in a ditch by the road down by Merkston's gas station. No identification. Nobody from round here. But somebody, I never did hear who, said they saw a black man in a beat-up pickup truck speedin' down the road near where that woman was found.

"Them Klan boys went round all the plantations and other places where colored live. Caught a couple fellas out in the street after dark. Chased one of 'em into the woods. They didn't catch him, but he ain't never been back round these parts since. The young boy they caught, they beat unmerciful. Only God knows why they didn't string him up. They might as well have. Boy wasn't fit for much after that. Broke his back. Put out one a his eyes. Hardly left him enough privates to make water." Nate shook his head mournfully from side to side.

"Well, it just so happen that round that time, I had me a ole piece of pickup truck. Them Klan boys spotted it in front of my place, tore my house up, and made somebody or another tell them where I was. Then they come here lookin' for me. I was out in front, seein' to them weeds in the flower bed when they drove up. They all jump out the truck wearin' them damn-fool outfits, callin' me out by name, and acting like the rabid dogs they is. They grabbed me and was draggin' me to they truck when Miz Grace come out the front door lookin' for me. Her dog, Lady, was 'bout to whelp and the child was 'spectin me to help with the birthin'.

"Miz Grace come runnin' over to those boys holdin' me. Now, you know what crackers is like round gentry, and these boys was just gettin' started, so they wasn't drunked up enough to step out they place. They stopped draggin' me off when the child come runnin', but they didn't let me go. 'This here your nigger, Miss?' one of 'em ask her.

"'Yes,' she told him, 'and you let him go right now! He has to stay here to see to my dog!' Just like that she said it, bold as brass. By this time, Miz Em heard the commotion and come to the door. 'What's going on here?' she wanted to know. That's when they let go a my arms, 'cause they had to take off them dummy caps and show some respect to their better. 'We lookin' for a nigger what run over a white woman with a beat-up pickup truck, ma'am.'

"'Well, this one's truck isn't working just now, but he is. For me. Nate, come see to the child's dog.' She beckoned for me to come in the house, right through the front door. She didn't take her eyes off them Klan boys till they was in the truck and headed down the drive."

By the time he got to this point in his story, Nate seemed to have slipped out from behind his protective wall. There was amusement, and something else she couldn't read, on his face when he turned to look directly at her for the first time since he'd begun speaking. "Minute I see Miz Grace agin, I tole her. I say, 'Miz Grace, I'm in your debt. I really is. Why, if you hadn't needed me to midwife your dog, I'd probably be dead today!'"

They looked at each other for a long moment, then broke into peals of laughter tinged with deep sorrow at his debt, which they both knew he did not take lightly, despite the circumstances under which it had been incurred. When they'd finally settled down, Nate began speaking again, almost as though he needed to tell a different tale in order to clear his mind of the one he'd just told.

"Back then, Mr. Everett's people owned the Lace Hill plantation over by Sheldon Road. Sheriff's folks was sharecroppers on Lace Hill. Mr. Everett and Miz Grace used to ride that fat pony of his up and down the road and play cowboys and Indians right out in them woods. That was 'fore Miz Grace went off to boardin' school and stopped comin' here for the summers, after her little cousin drowned in that same pond out front. Miz Grace was mighty upset 'bout that. There was a heap a gossip that didn't make no sense, but nobody never did figure out what that little girl was doin' out there that time a night. Miz Grace was real broke up over that business. She was the one that found the child. Never did get her spunk back, far as I can tell." The veil of memory lifted from Nate's eyes. He shifted in his chair. "That was a mighty fine glass of lemonade, Miz City."

Blanche took the hint and refilled his glass. He took a long swallow before he went on. "Now, Mr. Everett's daddy packed up his family and moved down Atlanta way in 1952. Wasn't no need to stay hereabouts. He lost Lace Hill to Kyle Munroe in a poker game." Nate shook his head in censure and took another swig of lemonade.

Blanche leaned back in her chair and adopted a listening pose. Nate had already proved to her that he was a storytelling man. She knew enough storytelling folks—like her Aunt Maeleen, who could bring tears to Blanche's eyes by telling her about the tragic death and/or funeral of someone neither of them knew—to know that a storytelling person couldn't be rushed. Their rhythm, the silences between their words, and their intonation were as important to the telling of the tale as the words they spoke. The story might sound like common gossip when told by another person, but in the mouth of a storyteller, gossip was art.

"...Course, them no-count Munroes didn't know doodly-squat 'bout runnin' no plantation. Killed the land and ended up sellin' it to developers who put up them tacky little houses for mill workers. That's how come Stillwell is the sheriff 'stead of sharecroppin' like his daddy." Nate leaned back in his chair.

"Mista Mumsfield come here 'bout six years back, after his folks was killed in a plane crash. Miz Em always did like the boy, even if he 'tarded. His daddy was Miz Em's favorite nephew. Then Miz Em broke her leg. That's why Miz Grace come up here from Atlanta. To look after her aunt and the boy. Or so they say. Miz Grace's daddy and Mr. Mumsfield's daddy was brothers, ya see.

Her daddy was a high-muckty-muck lawyer down Atlanta. Had a heart attack right in the courtroom! She was his only child. Left her a heap of money, but it's all gone now. Thanks to *him*. Don't seem to matter much to Miz Grace. She still crazy 'bout him."

"So the sheriff was friends with *him*, when they was coming up?" Blanche gave the same intonation to the word "him" that Nate himself had used. She was beginning to suspect that Nate planned to tell her everything about these people except why the sheriff was hanging around. She wondered why but was sure Nate would never respond to that question.

"*He* ain't never had no friends. Leastways not no men friends." Nate's mouth turned down at the corners. "Sheriff usta play with Mr. Everett and Miz Grace, till he got big enough to work in the fields with his daddy. Sheriff took a dislikin' to Mr. Everett after that."

Blanche wasn't surprised to learn that there was old bad blood between Everett and the sheriff, or that Everett needed more than one adoring fan at a time. She'd suspected from the lack of any papers, books, or briefcase among his things that he needed somebody to pay his way. "Does Grace know Everett's running around?"

"Lot she don't know 'bout him." Nate fell silent for a few moments in which he seemed to stare right through Blanche. "But some things she just got to know. Everybody know they own." He spoke in a slightly puzzled talking-to-himself tone.

Blanche repeated each of his words in her head but found no clue to what they collectively meant. "Maybe the sheriff is threatening to tell Grace about Everett running around. Maybe that's why he's hanging around here."

Nate gave her a quizzical frown. "Why he want to do that?" He shook his head vigorously from side to side. "Naw, Miz City. That ain't what it's 'bout."

"What is it about, then?" She tried to catch and hold his eyes, but he looked away before she could get a good grasp.

"Less we know 'bout it, the better. You remember what I say, now. Anybody ask you anything 'bout these people, just say you don't know nothin'. Nothin' at all!"

"Well, it wouldn't be a lie!" Now, she added to herself. She intended to change that situation. It was just so male of him to decide that he would withhold the juicy bits for her own good. It would be fun to teach him a lesson. She didn't doubt that she could find out what he was hiding. A family couldn't have domestic help and secrets. Fortunately, Nate was not her only source of information. Too bad Miz Minnie refused to have a phone in her house, but that problem was easily overcome. In the meantime, Nate could at least entertain her with some more common knowledge. "What about Mumsfield? You say he's been here six years?"

Nate slumped a little in his chair, relaxing into this easily answered question. "Why, I remember when Mista Mumsfield first come here to stay. Cried all the time, wouldn't talk to nobody. Miz Em pulled him outta hisself. Turned the limousine over to him...I don't know what the boy's goin' to do once..." Nate stopped in mid-sentence. Blanche watched him but said nothing.

"Best I be gittin' on. Sittin' round doin' a lotta loose talkin' don't get that garden tended." He gave Blanche a look that somehow blamed her for making him say more than he'd planned.

"What about the sheriff?" She asked more out of curiosity about how he'd react than in expectation of any information.

Nate set his now-empty glass in the sink, then leaned on the table and brought his face close to hers. His gaze was as piercingly direct as her own had been earlier. "Just keep your eyes down and your ears shut. Believe me, Miz City, that's the best thing for you round this place. And for me, too." His voice was serious and sad. He turned and walked toward the back door.

That's okay, she told herself with a smile, now determined to best him in the information-gathering department. She rose and looked out the window over the sink. Everett was hurrying toward the front of the house with a stiff, almost goosestepping gait. His fists were clenched. Next time, he'll explode, she thought. She could hear a car going quickly down the drive. Her body had already told her the coast was clear, the sheriff was gone. Blanche went to the phone.

"Ardell?" Blanche hurriedly told her friend about Nate's miserly information habits and how she planned to cure him.

"Sounds like a visit to Miz Minnie is in order," Ardell told her before Blanche could make the request. "I'll get right on it, honey. And you be careful! Sounds like you got some folks who're badly out of balance." Ardell was deep into being balanced and centered. Blanche agreed in principle but refused to give up a tilt toward excess every once in a while.

When she'd hung up, Blanche took lamb chops from the refrigerator and began trimming thick, pearly slabs of fat. She'd been planning to call Taifa and Malik after lunch, when she was sure they'd be back from church. Now she was just as eager to talk to Ardell.

Grace and Everett were bamboozling Mumsfield out of his money, or at least out of control of it. Not unusual behavior among the sort of people for whom she worked, especially if, as Nate said, Everett had already run through Grace's money and she'd bought him in the first place. Maybe her own money was just the down payment. Emmeline's clumsily covered up alcoholism was also typical of many families—rich and poor—who thought they could pretend reality away.

She washed and trimmed the green beans for steaming, roasted some pine nuts to go in them, and made a dressing for the melon salad. She decided to feed Emmeline before Everett. Grace and Mumsfield had gone into Farleigh to church. Grace wasn't having lunch, and Mumsfield would no doubt eat when they returned. Blanche cautioned herself to be cool as she prepared Emmeline's tray.

Once again, Emmeline didn't bother to answer when Blanche knocked on her door. She didn't acknowledge Blanche's presence, or that of the lunch tray Blanche put on the table at her elbow. The window curtains were still drawn and the bed covers hung half on the floor. Emmeline was propped up in the same chair she'd occupied yesterday. Her feet were bare, the toenails long and thick. The green satin robe that sagged from her shoulders was littered with ashes and dotted with tiny cigarette burns. And she stinks, Blanche remarked to herself. She made the bed and emptied Emmeline's ashtray.

"Shall I open the window, ma'am?"

"Get the hell out of here," Emmeline mumbled in a monotone. "And tell that bitch not to send you up to spy on me again, or I'll make her good and sorry."

Blanche stared at Emmeline, trying to see her through Mumsfield's eyes. Love, she thought, can truly make a princess out of a pig.

Blanche went back downstairs and served Everett's lunch. There was no hint of her growing distrust and dislike of the man in the solicitous way she offered him peas and scalloped potatoes, or in the flourish with which she presented the lamb chops and mint jelly. It was a game she sometimes played with herself when she particularly disliked an employer she couldn't afford to drop. She'd give herself merit points for being as correct and as civil as possible. The more discerning employer soon became aware of the insult implied by her overly polite behavior but could do nothing much about it. Had she been planning to stay in his employ, Everett would have come to understand that behind her meticulous care, she was prepared to nail his ass to the wall—at least verbally—if he ever again stretched her name out as though it were a piece of already chewed gum on the hands of a messy child. But it was questionable whether anything was getting through to Everett right now. Three times, as she served his meal, Everett had stared at his watch.

"Can I get you anything else, sir?"

Everett looked at his watch once again. "I've got one-fifteen. Is that the right ti—" He was out of his chair and headed for the phone while the first ring was still vibrating the air. Blanche followed him to the doorway and listened.

"Is everything all right? I've been waiting...What? What? Are you sure? Oh, God! Oh, God! No. I'm all right. It's just the shock. I...Yes, yes. But we'll have to tell her, ask her to...Of course. As soon as you get back. Yes. Goodbye."

Blanche ran to the table, spilled a few peas on it, and began cleaning them up. "Sorry, sir, I..." She started to speak, expecting him to come back, but he didn't return. She eased down the hall to the living room. Everett was pacing back and forth. "Excuse me, sir. Are you finished with lunch?"

He jumped at the sound of her voice, crossed the room, and threw himself into Grace's chair. "Yes. Clear it away." He rose as abruptly as he'd sat down. Blanche could hear him across the hall in the sitting room, the clink of glass against decanter as he poured himself a drink.

She wondered who'd been on the phone. At first, she'd been sure he was talking to Grace. But Everett had said, "I'm all right. It's just the shock." Blanche had never heard Grace ask after his welfare. It was generally he who asked after and took care of her. Could it have been the woman Everett was seeing? Whatever was said, it obviously wasn't anything Everett wanted to hear. Things might get real interesting when Grace came home. Blanche finished the lunch dishes and checked to see what Everett was up to. He was back in the living room, slumped in the same chair with his eyes closed and a glass of whiskey in his hand. Blanche went back to the kitchen. She cleared her mind of anything that might show up in her voice as worry, then dialed her mother's number.

For the first few minutes they talked about how the children were handling Blanche's being away. While this was far from the first time they'd been separated from her, this time was different, unplanned. No "Goodbye," "Bring me," or "Be good" had been said. Still, according to her mother, they seemed to be all right. Malik hadn't had any nightmares, which was how he showed his upsets, and Taifa hadn't picked any more fights than usual with her friends, which was her way. Mama, too, sounded fine. Of course, with Mama, sounding fine meant making a fuss.

"Now, you listen to me, Blanche. You act like you got some sense, you hear me? This ain't no time for bein' uppity." She spoke in her most no-nonsense voice. "You just smile with your mouth closed and those people won't pay you no mind."

"Yes, Mama." Blanche stifled the impulse to ask her how she'd come to be an expert on hiding out in other people's houses. "Mama, I really appreciate how you—"

"I'm not foolin' with you, girl," Miz Cora interrupted. "You do like I say and behave yourself and don't let that mouth of yours git you in trouble. And give me that phone number this minute! I got a right to talk to my own child, even if she is wanted by the police and livin' with some white folks, out in the middle of God knows where! I sure will be glad when that darned check comes, so you can git…"

Blanche let her mother talk longer than was wise, but she knew Miz Cora needed to fuss at her as much as Blanche needed the reassurance of her mother's voice.

Just as Blanche was about to interrupt, her mother seemed to read her mind. "…And that Cora Lee Walters come by here a while ago. Thinkin' she was gon' take my grandbabies on over to that cold old house of hers. But I told her, 'No, ma'am, even though you is their poor dead daddy's mama. Not today. We got plans,' I told her. I just had a feelin' you'd be callin' 'bout now.

"Taifa! Malik! It's Mama Blanche!" she shouted.

"When you coming home, Mama Blanche? And where did you say you were?" Taifa asked in her most officious tone.

"Mama! Mama!" Malik shouted in Blanche's ear.

Then her mother's voice in the background: "Boy! You know I don't tolerate no brute force! Give that phone back to your sister and wait your turn!"

When Taifa came back on the line, she told Blanche about the fish she'd caught the day before and how Uncle Leo said she and Malik were almost as good at fishing as he was. Blanche silently thanked the child for not continuing to ask when she'd be home.

When Malik got his turn to talk, he was still miffed about being chastised, but he cheered up as they talked. "...And I helped row the boat, too!" he told her, then wound his way through the fishing trip, and his friend Donnell's fall from his bike, which had resulted in a chipped tooth.

Blanche hated the fact that while they talked, she was distracted by the realization of how long she'd been on the phone. But, as with her mother, she let the children rattle on. In reward, she found herself laughing without irony for the first time since she'd left home three days ago. They passed the phone back and forth until they finally worked their way back around to where they'd begun, with questions about her return home. She took a deep breath and told them she wasn't sure when they'd be together again, but that it might be a while. In the silence that followed, she told them, as she rarely did at home, how much she loved them. She sent them kisses and hugs and reminded them to take good care of their grandmother.

When her mother came back on the line, Blanche could hardly talk around her tears. Her mother had something to say about that, once she sent Malik and Taifa out to play. "You ain't got no energy to waste on snivelin', girl. You got your front and your back to watch. I didn't raise you to be neither weaklin' nor fool. Now you stop that cryin' and act like you got some backbone!"

"Yes, Mama. Bye, Mama." Despite her mother's orders, Blanche hurried into the laundry room off the kitchen and turned on the tap in the utility tub to muffle her sobs. Unlike her mother, Blanche believed in tears. She knew from long experience how cleansing and calming a good cry could be. And she had more than herself to cry about. The memory of the silence that had followed her announcement to the kids made her cry even harder. After her tears came those restful moments in which whatever she'd been crying about was clearly understood to be outside of herself, some flaw in the world, not in her, and therefore not insurmountable. It was a state that made it possible for her to prepare and serve a dinner that showed no signs of her distress. She washed the asparagus and tried to decide whether to cook enough so that there'd be some left over for a vegetable soufflé on Monday—she found that leftover asparagus worked much better in her soufflé than fresh. She looked up as Mumsfield approached the kitchen.

She made him a couple of smoked turkey sandwiches to hold him until dinner and hoped he wouldn't linger. She was still brimming over with her own feelings and in no mood to talk. But he was.

"And may the Lord God bless you one and all," he told her in a deep, pompously ministerial voice, with an oversized grin on his face. He went on to mimic some of his fellow churchgoers, including the less than kind comments they made about others among them—comments made right in front of him, because his condition made him as invisible as her color and profession made her.

"We went to our house, Blanche. But Cousin Grace made me wait in the car. I only wanted to get my baseball cap. Why wouldn't she let me go in the house with her, Blanche?"

"Umm hmm." Blanche nodded her head and sighed.

"Are you tired, Blanche?" Mumsfield asked her.

Blanche felt her face flush. She didn't like to half-listen when someone talked to her. She was too well acquainted with how it felt to be treated as though what she said wasn't worth the energy it took to listen.

"I'm sorry, Mumsfield, honey. Maybe you could tell me all about it some other time. I just can't set my mind to it right now." As she spoke, she prepared herself for his feeling rejected.

Instead, Mumsfield cocked his head to the side as though trying to listen harder, or to make sure he understood what she'd said. Then he gave her one of the sweetest smiles Blanche had ever seen.

"Yes, Blanche. I will tell you tomorrow. I trust you, Blanche. You know I understand things." He left the kitchen for the front of the house.

She was glad his feelings weren't hurt because she'd told him to leave off with his church story, and she understood why he was so pleased that she'd told him so, instead of pretending an interest she didn't have. All us invisibles are probably sensitive about that, she thought.

Dinner was a quick and quiet affair. Blanche had hoped some clue as to what that phone conversation was about would come out at dinner while she was in the room, but Grace and Everett hardly spoke, each seeming preoccupied with unshared thoughts. If there was any conversation beyond that related to passing dishes back and forth, it didn't take place while Blanche was in the room.

True to his word, the next morning Mumsfield was in the kitchen well before breakfast, and still full of his trip to town and to church yesterday. Blanche was ready for him, this time. She'd slept well and woken to the lucky song of a mockingbird. While she'd brushed her teeth and bathed, she'd bucked up her spirits with speculations about what she would find in Boston besides cold weather.

Now she gave Mumsfield her full attention. She laughed as he moved his hands in the air, sketching women's hats that should never have been made, let alone worn, and demonstrated the strut of importance practiced by the husbands. Then he sang his favorite bits of several hymns. She realized that everything was still exciting and fresh to him. It didn't matter that he'd probably heard those hymns and seen those hats many times before. It was enough for him that church and hats existed. Things didn't have to be unique to be interesting. She envied him his baby eyes, his ability to find delight in the simple parts of life. It made her wonder about the term "retarded."

But even though she could tell Mumsfield was pleased with the conversation, she still sensed a watchfulness in him, as though he were observing her for signs of inattentiveness or boredom. She showed none. She asked him for details of the church and the state of traffic. She liked talking to him. She liked trying to see the world the way he saw it. She was sure talking to him was good for her.

After breakfast, she vacuumed and dusted the living room and dining room and moved upstairs. When she'd finished making beds in all the other rooms, she stopped in front of Emmeline's door.

"I won't! I won't!" Emmeline shouted just as Blanche knocked on the door. Blanche fully expected to be politely turned away by Grace, or shouted at and told to "stay the hell out" by Emmeline herself. But this morning, Grace waved her inside and went to stand with her back to the window. The place looked and smelled like what it was, a room constantly occupied by a person sweating gin. Blanche wished she could open a window but assumed if they'd wanted one open, they'd have done so. She worked as quickly as she could. It wasn't just the smelly, messy room that made her hurry. The silent fight going on between Emmeline and Grace was like red-hot pincers on Blanche's nerves. She could feel their wills rolling around the room, scratching and clawing at each other like two characters out of that old *Gang Girls in Prison* movie. All the while their eyes were riveted on her. Grace was poised on the balls of her feet, ready to speak or act should Emmeline say or do the wrong thing. Emmeline lay limp in her chair, her body almost melding with the upholstery. No part of her moved, except her hard, bloodshot eyes, which gleamed with alertness. Blanche thought it was the pose of a person who knew how to use other people's strength to her own advantage. She also realized that while Grace and Emmeline kept their eyes on her, she was just the lens through which they eyed each other suspiciously. She was relieved when she had to move on to the connecting bathroom.

From the condition of the tub, it seemed that Emmeline had finally had a bath. In Blanche's experience, it was unusual for a woman in Grace's position to attend to the washing of wrinkled old behinds. Of course, from the way the old lady had smelled yesterday, Grace wasn't doing such a hot job. Still, it was odd that they didn't hire a nurse or companion for Emmeline, or at least try to foist more of her care onto the help. At first, it had seemed kind of nice that Grace chose to personally care for her aunt. Now Blanche knew there was very little that was nice going on between them. She finished off the bathroom with a swipe at the mirror over the basin and left Emmeline's bedroom without a word to either of the silent women.

It was later that day that Mumsfield told Blanche about the clothes in the guest room next to Emmeline's room.

SEVEN

B lanche moved around the kitchen preparing to prepare dinner—gathering bowls and large wooden spoons, choosing knives, setting out measuring cups. She paused in her search for a large colander when she heard Mumsfield calling her name. He said it three times before he ever got to the kitchen—at least she hoped he was saying it out loud and that she wasn't picking it up from his thoughts.

"Blanche," he said again, as he entered the room. His voice was full of questions and rose slightly with each repetition of her name. "Who is in the guest room, Blanche?"

"I don't know, Mumsfield, honey." Blanche found the colander and turned her attention to looking for a ring mold for the rice. "Who do you think is in there?" she asked after she'd located the pan on a pull-out shelf in a cabinet beside the stove.

"No one is in the guest room, Blanche. No one."

She wasn't accustomed to Mumsfield not making sense, so she was halted for a few seconds. She looked at him closely to make sure he was all right. His perpetually quizzical eyes gazed steadily back at her.

"You mean the guest-room person isn't in the guest room now?" she half-stated, half-asked. She nodded with satisfaction when Mumsfield agreed with her interpretation.

"When did you see the person in the guest room?" She was once again stopped by Mumsfield's answer.

"Never, Blanche. I never saw the person in the guest room."

Blanche decided to try a different direction. "Mumsfield, honey, what were you doing in the guest room?" For a moment, she thought he wasn't going to answer. He blinked in a way that made her think he might be about to cry. She'd decided to tell him to forget the question, when he started speaking. His voice was soft and hesitant.

"Sometimes," he began, "sometimes..." He shook his head, as if to clear it. "Sometimes, I touch...I feel Aunt Emmeline here," he said, holding his hand up, as though he were about to press his palm against something. "I go in the...in the guest room...in the closet. I put my hand..." Once again, he raised his hand as though to press it against a wall, then sighed deeply. "But there was no feeling, Blanche. No feeling. Only the clothes." His sadness brimmed out of his eyes and made his mouth quiver.

Blanche understood what Mumsfield was trying to tell her about the feeling between him and Emmeline. Blanche had shared the same kind of super-sensitivity with her girlhood friend Eula, a high-yellow, sweet-faced girl who'd been Blanche's other self for the two years Eula had lived with her aunt and uncle in a house three doors from Blanche's own. Blanche and Eula's twin-hood was sealed by their both beginning to menstruate on the same rainy spring day. Blanche's heart had nearly broken when her mother told her Eula's uncle and aunt had been killed in an accident, and Eula was being sent back to her parents and fifteen brothers and sisters in Florida. She'd never found a friend to replace Eula, not even Ardell.

Now Blanche took Mumsfield's hand and led him to a chair at the table. She fetched him a glass of lemonade and sat across from him and waited until thoughts of his aunt were no longer creases in his forehead.

"Now," she said, "how do you know someone's been in the guest room?"

"The clothes, Blanche, I told you. The clothes. In the closet!"

"Aah." She asked him as many questions as she could think of about the color, shape, size, and texture of these clothes. When he'd finished answering her questions, she knew the clothes in the closet in the guest room were women's clothes that most likely belonged to Emmeline. Mumsfield's account of the shoes made her sure they were Enna Jetticks. Not Grace's type, yet.

Blanche wondered why Grace would put a complete set of Emmeline's clothes in the guest room. It wasn't likely to have been anyone else. Emmeline was usually so drunk Blanche had never seen her even stand up, although that didn't mean she couldn't. It was unlikely that Everett was well enough acquainted with old ladies' dressing habits to know to assemble snuggies and an undershirt as well as the usual slip, panties, and bra, especially this time of year. Something else for the list of peculiar things happening in this house, she thought.

"I don't know who's been in the guest room, Mumsfield, honey, but I think the clothes probably belong to your Aunt Emmeline."

Mumsfield broke into full smile. He could, as he'd said last night, understand things. You only needed to get in step with his way of putting his thoughts and words together, just as you had to squint to read fine print.

Mumsfield switched the subject to what was for dinner and spent the next hour learning the intricacies of making a good wild rice ring.

Blanche had hoped to slip up the back stairs to put away some of the laundry she'd done after breakfast, but talking to Mumsfield had put her behind. She checked the thermometer in the veal roast and basted it with the pan juices.

After dinner, Grace brought Emmeline's tray back to the kitchen. From the looks of the plate, Emmeline had, as usual, eaten very little.

"Your cooking is quite good, Blanche." Grace set the tray on the table and turned to Blanche.

"Quite good," my foot, Blanche thought. "Fabulous" is more like it. But she merely nodded her all-purpose nod, which could be interpreted to mean whatever the viewer needed it to mean.

"You must have had a fine teacher."

"Yes, ma'am."

Blanche knew Grace intended for her to say on, to talk about how she'd learned to cook and from whom. But Blanche didn't want to play the let's-pretend-I'm-interested-in-you-as-a-person game. It might be necessary to Grace's image of herself, but even to keep a low profile Blanche wasn't prepared to go along with the go-long, as Cousin Murphy used to say.

"Have you considered a regular cook's position?"

"I can't stand the constant heat, ma'am. Makes me all dizzy and nauseous." She managed to keep a straight face somehow. Her sarcasm was totally wasted on Grace who arranged her features into a mask of sympathetic understanding, as though Blanche had said she couldn't be a cook because of some disability. Blanche coughed down the laugh that threatened to betray her. Grace, having discharged her duty to show personal interest in the help, went on to talk about what really concerned her. Blanche both listened to and watched her as she issued her velvet-sheathed orders.

"We like our bed linen changed every three days this time of year." Grace was flushed, her eyes bright and alert. She spoke with a crispness Blanche had first heard when Grace had opened the back gate to admit Blanche to the house in town. The last time Grace had seemed so sure of herself was when they'd done the meal planning. She's in her element, Blanche thought. For all her rattled, nearly helpless behavior, she likes being in charge. She really believes she's the Mistress of the Manor. Is that why she wants to control Mumsfield's money, to make sure she gets to play *châtelaine* in high style? Although, from what Blanche had overheard, the will-changing business sounded like Everett's idea.

"And please remember, just a hint of starch in Mr. Everett's shirts."

For one brief moment, their eyes actually met. Blanche was the first to look away. "Yes, ma'am."

After Grace left the kitchen, Blanche sat down at the table. Was it just that old race thing that had thrown her off when her eyes met Grace's? Her neighbor Wilma's father said he'd never in his adult life looked a white person in the eye. He'd grown up in the days when such an act very often ended in a black person's charred body swinging from a tree. For many years, Blanche worried that it was fear which sometimes made her reluctant to meet white people's eyes, particularly on days when she had the loneliest or the unspecified blues. She'd come to understand that her desire was to avoid pain, a pain so old, so deep, its memory was carried not in her mind, but in her bones. Some days she simply didn't want to look into the eyes of people likely raised to hate, disdain, or fear anyone who looked like her. It was not always useful to be in touch with race memory. The thought of her losses sometimes sucked the joy from her life for days at a time.

But in this case, it was Grace's particular eyes that she'd shied away from. There'd been something in them that was all Grace, which Blanche hadn't wanted to see. She was still sitting at the table when Grace returned to the kitchen.

Now Grace's eyes were wide and red-rimmed. They flitted around the room like trapped birds. Her hands were clenched tightly together, her knuckles stood out sharp and white as bleached bones. Blanche wondered if she'd imagined Grace's calm assurance of a few minutes ago. "Please take the two... gentlemen on the side porch some refreshments." She spoke more slowly than usual, and, given her appearance and behavior, Blanche was surprised by her even tone of voice.

Blanche fetched napkins, filled a cut-glass pitcher with iced tea, and set it on a large serving tray along with a decanter of brandy, snifters, and tall, thin iced tea glasses. She could feel, and sometimes see, Grace's eyes on her. They reminded Blanche of a storm she'd once seen building out to sea. The clouds had tumbled soundlessly end over end in the distance, gathering around the heart of the storm. When the storm broke over the beach it had flattened everything it touched. Where was Everett? Why wasn't he playing host to these two gentlemen who'd caused such a reaction in Grace?

Curiosity lightened Blanche's step as she moved through the house. She balanced the tray on her hip while she opened the door and stepped out onto the screened-in porch. There was still some light in the sky, but on the porch deep shadows had already begun to settle in for the night. As she was about to round the corner onto the long side porch, one of the men spoke. Blanche relaxed and imagined her ears to be large, trumpet-shaped organs designed to pick up the smallest sound. What she heard made it clear that the men on the porch were neither gentle nor strangers.

"Bobbie Lee, I don't have that kind of money. And even if I did..."

"'Even if I did,' my ass! You still don't seem to understand what's goin' on here, Everett, ole buddy! I've got you by the short hairs. I can pull your whole life apart with just a few words in the right places, and there ain't jackshit you can do about it but pay up!" The sheriff's voice was full of confidence.

"Who the hell do you think you are, speaking to me like this!" Everett's voice cracked in mid-sentence, like tree bark in a forest fire.

"Can that, ole buddy. You just get my money. That's all you got to do. Or I talk."

"Do you really think he's going to take a chance on ruining his career for a miserable fifty thousand?" Everett's tone made it clear what he thought of the possibility.

"I know he will," the sheriff told him. "He's got his own problems. But that ain't none of your business. You just get the cash."

One of the men struck a match.

"Listen, I've got a lot of connections in and around Atlanta. People who owe me favors. I could get you fixed up down there. You could leave this place, forget about…"

A whiff of cigar smoke wrinkled Blanche's nose.

"We've been through that. I ain't goin' nowhere. I'm the sheriff of this here county, and I like being the sheriff of this county just fine. And that's just the way I intend for things to stay. I ain't leavin' here for some two-bit clerkin' job or drivin' some damn truck! And I ain't about to lose this job!"

When Everett spoke, his voice was so low Blanche had to lean forward to hear it. "You ought to think it over, Sheriff," he said. "Sometimes it's better to run than to stay and fight." All the uncertain boyishness was gone from his voice, replaced by something much more adult and dangerous.

The sheriff laughed. "Everett, you ain't got the balls to make good on that threat." The sheriff's voice wasn't quite as sure as his words.

The sound of one of the men walking toward her end of the porch set Blanche in motion. She turned the corner and set the tray on a small table between two white-painted rattan chairs. She looked at the two men from the corner of her eye. They'd both discovered a deep interest in looking out at the pond. They ignored her, except that they didn't speak while she was present.

She longed to listen from around the corner on her way back to the kitchen, but Grace might be waiting there for her, wondering what was taking her so long. If she got caught eavesdropping, and the sheriff remembered where it was that he'd recently seen her…Still, she waited a few more moments, but she couldn't outwait their silence.

Grace was gone from the kitchen when Blanche returned, but the air was still heavy with her presence. Blanche moved about with the automatic movements of the domestic robot of many women's dreams, while her mind went about its own affairs.

She wiped the countertops with more elbow grease than was warranted, and wondered what story Everett would tell Grace in order to get the money for the sheriff, as Blanche was sure he would. If Grace dumped him, he might have to make his own way in the world. That would never do. Blanche folded and refolded the dish towel until its ends met perfectly. She set the chairs just so in relation to the table. What a household! More slipping and sliding than a drunk on ice skates. She'd been more right about the sheriff and Everett than Nate had given her credit for, but she still had no idea what Nate was hiding. She wished she could have a good long talk with Miz Minnie instead of having to wait for Ardell's report. It would do her good to talk with Miz Minnie.

In an African history and culture course she'd taken at the Freedom Library, back in the sixties, Blanche had learned that among some African peoples, there were wise women elders who chose the chiefs and counseled them. Had Miz Minnie been born among such a people, she would undoubtedly have been one of those women. Miz Minnie knew a good portion of the private affairs of practically every black person in her community. In times of trouble, almost everyone found themselves talking with Miz Minnie. Some folks just went to see her, and spilled their pain out on her scrubbed wooden floors and handmade rag rugs, and let her soothe them with wise words and sassafras tea. Other people met her seemingly by accident and found themselves telling all their business, although they'd never planned to do such a thing. Everyone came away fortified. Blanche could just see her in her grease-stained cotton house dress, mincing along on fat-heeled feet in oversized men's bedroom shoes, hard-pressed hair done up in greasy gray curls that peeked out from under her ever-present head scarf, her lower lip packed with snuff.

Because she knew the black community, Miz Minnie also had plenty of information about the white one. Blanche wondered if people who hired domestic help had any idea how much their employees learned about them while fixing their meals, making their beds, and emptying their trash. Did it ever occur to the kind of women for whom she worked that they and their lives were often topics of conversation and sometimes objects of ridicule or pity among the help's friends and families? She locked the back door and went to the front of the house to see if anyone wanted anything else before she went up to bed.

In the middle of another dream about buses—hundreds and thousands of buses zooming up a steep hill, their tires humming like a million bumblebees—she was suddenly wide awake. She didn't need to go to the toilet, she wasn't thirsty, and all was quiet. But the half-memory of a dull thump flickered in a corner of her mind. She separated the cacophony of a country night into its various parts: crickets rubbing their hind legs together, frogs inflating their throats, a faint breeze in the boughs of the pine trees, the sound of something rolling slowly over gravel.

She flung back the covers and scrambled out of bed. She was out the door of her room and down the hall as fast as she could move. She made it to the window in time to see the limousine rolling down the drive, lights and motor off.

There was something dreamlike about the scene out the window. The almost fluorescent pink azalea blossoms were pale lights floating in the dark. The car was densely black against the silvery green foliage. A slow-moving monster sneaking up on somebody, she thought.

As she watched, the driver lowered the window, put an elbow on the windowsill, then leaned out and looked back at the house. The moonlight streamed into the opened window and struck Everett full in the face just before the limousine was swallowed by the deeper darkness beneath the trees that lined the drive. When he reached the bottom of the drive, he turned on the headlights. The treetops made lace doilies against the sky.

Of course, there was no sleep waiting for her when she got back to bed. She lay staring at the square of midnight blue out her window.

Everett was probably on his way to tell his lady friend that they were on the verge of being exposed if he didn't pay the sheriff off. Blanche wondered who the woman was. Probably someone with whom Grace was friendly, if not a close friend of hers. Blanche had seen it so many times it no longer amazed her—people too rich to worry about being fired from their jobs or evicted from their homes who seemed to seek the threat of total disaster that poor people sought to avoid. They achieved this state of risk by screwing their husband's brother or their wife's closest friend. Blanche had watched bored, listless employers grow energetic and bright-eyed from the thrill of putting the horns on their mates with the help of someone who was a part of their intimate circle. Blanche shook her head and sucked her teeth and eventually drifted off to sleep.

EIGHT

In the morning, Blanche fiddled with the radio dial until she found a station that promised news. Most mornings, she tried to listen to the news before she left for work. But most mornings, she was too busy pressing a dress for Taifa to wear to school, polishing Malik's shoes, and getting herself ready to go to work to give more than half an ear to the early-morning news. This morning, making biscuits for her employers' breakfast was the distraction. It took her a few moments to understand what the man was saying. She stopped in the middle of forming the biscuit dough into a ball and turned to stare at the radio as though it were a television set. Her hands hung limply over the bowl. Bits of dough clung to her fingers.

"...said the sheriff's apparent suicide may be linked to the investigation. More news at ten, right here on..."

All the tension in Blanche's neck and back drained away at once. She was momentarily light-headed. She leaned against the table to steady herself. He won't be asking me no more questions. She poured a bit more milk into the bowl and squeezed the dough into a moist blob. She waited for the pang, like a string breaking, that she always felt when she heard of the death of someone she knew. It didn't come. She turned the now springy dough out onto a marble cutting board and kneaded it. The dough took on life, growing more springy and responsive beneath her hands. One less enemy in the world, she thought. One less racist. She rolled the dough out.

He hadn't simply died. The news report said he'd committed suicide. "I ain't going nowhere. Nowhere at all," he'd told Everett just last night. Why would a man who was just talking about how he wanted to continue to live in a certain place up and kill himself the very same night, or early the next morning? The perfect dough floated from the biscuit cutter onto the baking sheet. Blanche wished she'd lingered on the front porch a little longer last night. As it was, the last thing she'd heard Everett utter was a threat against the sheriff. Then Everett goes out in the middle of the night and the sheriff is dead in the morning. She stopped what she was doing and laid her hand across her stomach, as if she could press away the warning hollowness behind her diaphragm. She was staying in a house with a murderer. She was also running from the law. The sheriff had found her yesterday, and this morning he had turned up dead.

She opened the oven door and placed the biscuits inside. If the rest of the world decided that the sheriff had been murdered, she was a prime suspect. If she were to run and be caught now, who knew what kind of trumped-up charges they'd hang on her? She was positive that all concerned would rather have her arrested for killing the sheriff than Everett.

Of course, it was possible the sheriff had killed himself. Life could certainly take the kind of quick and serious turn for the worse that made a person do things they had never thought they would. It had happened to her a number of times, including a few days ago. Had it really only been five days since she had taken off from the courthouse, heading in what was turning out to be a very wrong direction? She set the timer for twelve minutes.

She wondered if Grace knew. More likely, he'd done it to keep her from finding out what the sheriff knew. To keep his meal ticket safe. It would be better to forget about the sheriff's visits, his conversations with Everett, and the limousine rolling silently down the drive. That shouldn't be a problem. She had plenty of experience not seeing what went on in her customers' homes, like black eyes, specks of white powder left on silver-backed mirrors, cufflinks with the wrong initials under the bed, and prescriptions for herpes. She was particularly good at not seeing anything that might be dangerous or illegal. But as good as she was at being blind, there were certain things she couldn't overlook. She'd made more than one anonymous call to a non-custodial parent about child abuse.

But no helpless child was endangered by the sheriff's murder. Still, it tugged at her. She transferred plump, golden biscuits from the oven to a bun warmer. How had Everett made it look like suicide? She gathered eggs and milk, and scrambled them in butter, together with salt, pepper, and a dash of Tabasco. She imagined pills in some whiskey, a hose from the exhaust pipe to the front vent window of the sheriff's car, a blow to the head, poison, a bullet to the brain.

She carried the biscuits into the dining room along with the chafing dish of eggs, then the warmer of bacon and sausages. All the family members were at the table, except Emmeline, who, Blanche suspected, never came downstairs—at least not while she was in her cups. Blanche concentrated on the food to keep from staring at Everett calmly sipping his coffee. She felt as transparent as plastic wrap. Surely he knew that she knew, that she'd seen him, was a danger to him.

"Good morning, Blanche." Mumsfield grinned between spoonfuls of cornflakes.

Both Grace and Everett looked up at her. Everett's glance was quick and distracted. Grace moved her head so slowly she was like a woman under water. They both responded to Blanche's greeting with nods—Everett's curt, Grace's slow and careful, as though her head might roll off if she didn't move gingerly.

Blanche put the bread warmer and other dishes on the sideboard. She moved bowls and utensils about, cleared the grapefruit plates, and watched Everett from the corner of her eye. His eyes looked squinched together. Like something worrisome is tugging at them from the inside, she thought. In her mind, she heard him warning the sheriff in a voice as soft as a scorpion slipping across sand. She saw him sitting in the limousine as it rolled slowly and silently down the drive, the moonlight turning his already pale skin to vampire blue. And now the sheriff was dead. She stifled her strong longing for the privacy of the kitchen and braced herself to serve him. She was grateful when he waved her away. But before he did, she noticed that despite his almost constant sipping, his coffee cup was still full. And while he was holding his head as though reading the newspaper that lay beside his plate, he was actually watching his wife. Grace looked so limp she might have been loosely stuffed with sawdust. Her complexion was shallow, her face yellow as a harvest moon. She still had on her bedroom slippers and her legs were bare. She knows, Blanche thought, and was glad Everett was not her man. Grace took a dab of eggs and a slice of bacon but didn't eat them. Mumsfield speared massive quantities of bacon and sausages, three biscuits, and a large scoop of scrambled eggs.

But why was she so sure about Everett and the sheriff? She fished around in the dishwater for stray utensils. There was a dishwasher, of course, but it helped her to think things through when the front of her mind was distracted by some simple task. People threatened each other all the time. It didn't usually come to murder. Just because she'd seen Everett sneaking out of the house on the night the sheriff died didn't necessarily mean he was a murderer. She knew from Nate that Everett was running around on Grace. When she really thought about it, she had no concrete reason to suspect Everett, and no reason to think the sheriff's death was anything other than what the radio had said—suicide. But she did think. She'd lived too long to rely only on concrete evidence to tell her whether something was true. She thought it was likely the sheriff had found a way out of his investigation trouble other than his own death. She thought the sheriff's solution included paying someone off with money he expected to get from Everett for not telling Grace that Everett was fucking around. Blackmail, in a word. Blanche quickly searched her mind for the other word, the one that began with "ex." She tried not to use words that made black sound bad. When she couldn't find the word she wanted, she settled on "white male" and was pleased with how much more accurately her word described the situation. She used the spray attachment to give the dishes a final scalding rinse.

She twirled the dial on the radio, skating across music, talk shows, and commercials in search of some news. She looked over her shoulder at the wall clock. Nine-forty-five, three minutes later than it had been the last time she'd checked the clock. There wasn't likely to be any news before ten. She turned off the radio and let the dishwater out of the sink. Out the window, she saw Nate hobbling past the vegetable garden toward the back door. She wiped her hands on her apron and got the door open before he had a chance to knock. She stepped back to let him enter.

"Hear 'bout the sheriff?" he asked her without a "Hello" or "How are you?" He didn't even wait for Blanche to answer. "Shame, ain't it?" he added. But the huge grin that turned his face into that of a much younger, more carefree man didn't match his words.

It was probably events like the sheriff's death that got her slave ancestors a reputation for being happy, childlike, and able to grin in the face of the worst disaster. She could just see some old slaver trying to find a reason why the slaves did a jig when the overseer died.

"What happened?" She pulled a chair out from the table. Nate sat down and fanned himself with his battered baseball cap.

"Run his car off Oman's Bluff—'bout three miles down Kerry Road." He motioned with his head toward the east. "Exploded." He paused again. Blanche sank slowly into the chair across from him.

"They say he was stealing money hand over fist. Course, ain't nobody surprised to hear that." Nate chewed on the inside of his cheek and looked at Blanche from the corner of his eye.

Something's wrong, Blanche thought. Nate's a storytelling man. He'd no more walk in here and start spouting off the facts of an event like this than Aunt Mabel, who was generally considered the best-dressed woman in her church, would go to Sunday service in beat-up bedroom shoes.

Nate fiddled with his hat. His dark hands were as knotted as tree roots. His tan nails were edged with soil. He crossed and uncrossed his legs. "They say," he went on, still looking at Blanche from the corner of his eye, "they say he killed hisself 'cause it was all gon' be in the newspaper, 'bout him stealing, I mean." He stopped, turned his entire upper body to face her, and stared at her with perplexed, worried eyes. "But why would somebody from this here house be leavin' the very place where it happened? Couldn't have been nobody else!" he added quickly, as though she'd disagreed with him. "Ain't nobody else in these parts got a pink jacket." He said the words "pink jacket" in a way that made it clear what he thought of such a garment. Blanche said nothing. She knew there was more.

"I ain't slept much these last five or so years." Nate squeezed his cap between both hands as he spoke. "Most nights find me roamin' round my old place, my old yard. Just thinking 'bout things and…and bein' there, if you know what I mean. Sleep don't seem like the best way to use time when you ain't got but a drop or two left."

He looked out the window for a moment. What must he know? she wondered. What must he have learned, after all these years spent so close to the earth? She imagined evenings of listening to him talk of times gone and what they'd counted for.

"Some nights, I just sit out on my porch in the dark. Just sit and rock a bit. That's how I come to see that pink jacket. I live over by Kerry Road…not too far from Oman's Bluff, where the sheriff…where the sheriff died.

"Fact is," he added with a deep, shuddering sigh, "the shortcut to Oman's Bluff goes right by my front yard, right there 'cross the road from my front yard. A big ole pine branch fell on that path day 'fore yesterday. Anybody walkin' along the path got to step round that limb."

Nate hesitated once again. He wiped his hand across his face. "My eyes ain't all they once was, but when he stepped off the path to go round that there pine limb, I saw that pink jacket clear as..." His eyes widened slightly as he looked up from Blanche's face to the doorway beyond her.

Mumsfield, Blanche said to herself.

"And the carrots lookin' mighty fine, too." Nate was still looking over Blanche's head. He rose from the chair.

"Mornin', Mista Mumsfield." Nate eased toward the back door as he spoke.

Blanche turned her head. Mumsfield was standing with his head just inside the swinging door. "Hello, Nate. Hello, Blanche." Mumsfield came fully into the room. His voice was barely audible. He stood with his head hung, his eyes lowered, and his hands jammed deep in his pockets.

"Well, I best be seein' to them vegetables." Nate wished Mumsfield another "Good morning," gave Blanche a nod and a look she couldn't read, then slipped out the back door.

Blanche turned in her chair and stared at Mumsfield. Her usually soft brown eyes snapped with annoyance—once again, she'd felt his presence before her eyes or ears had any information to go on. Like he's some kind of kin of mine, she thought, and the thought irritated her.

She suddenly saw her affection for people as a wide lake whose sides sloped down to a very deep middle. Some people— Mama, the kids, Ardell, Cousin Maxine, and Blanche's New York buddy Carla Sanchez—floated in the middle of the lake. Lots of other people—neighbors she'd had over the years, schoolmates, old lovers, and such—waded in the shallower waters of her affection. But she knew that, when necessary, she could sweep unwanted waders right off her beach, including this one. She gave Mumsfield a hard look. I won't be here much longer, she reminded herself.

Mumsfield called her back to his immediate distress with a sigh damp with approaching tears. "Mumsfield is very sad, Blanche," he told her, as though she'd asked him a question. "Mumsfield heard Uncle Everett tell Aunt Grace about…about…"

"The sheriff?" Blanche asked him. Mumsfield raised his head and looked at her with tear-glazed eyes. Blanche almost burst out laughing. She manufactured a cough and politely covered her mouth with her hand. She turned away from Mumsfield until she straightened out her face. She didn't want him to think she was laughing at him, when her laughter was really a celebration of her own good sense. Hadn't she just been warning herself off this young man? Now here was a perfect example of why. Crying over the sheriff!

"Everyone dies, Mumsfield, honey." She tried to make her voice as gentle as possible. She rose, led him to a chair, and patted his shoulder while he sobbed softly into his cupped hands. Her mouth tightened into a plump line of disapproval toward a family in which a member had to come to the hired help for solace.

When Mumsfield's sobs had dissolved into shudders and sniffles, she questioned him about his relationship with the sheriff. From what he told her, it sounded as though the sheriff had hardly ever spoken to Mumsfield, beyond "Hello" and "Goodbye."

It's the sheriff of America-the-make-believe he's mourning, she told herself. Boy's been watching too much television.

By the time she'd finished explaining that death is what comes after life, the same way youth follows childhood, and how perfectly it seems to work to keep people and planet alive, Mumsfield was dry-eyed and attentive. He sat with his hands folded on the table like a student at a desk, until he was soothed and ready to go about his business.

Once he'd gone, Blanche hurried around the kitchen, making tea and toast and cooking two tablespoons of grits with milk to go with the eggs she was about to scramble for Emmeline's breakfast. It was nearly ten-thirty. Any second now, Grace would be along for the tray. On their first day in this house, Grace had said she would take Emmeline's meals up herself. Blanche wasn't assuming that had changed just because she'd been called on to deliver them twice.

When the toast began to wilt, Blanche went looking for Grace. She found Everett in the hall, just hanging up the phone. His back was toward her and he seemed unaware of her presence. She wondered if he was as rare as he ought to have been. She worked among people who thought they owned the world. It was likely that others of them at least thought they had the right to do what this one had done. He ruffled his hair, then brushed it back with graceful, long-fingered hands. His movements were less rigid than when he had been with the sheriff. More upset than angry, she thought.

"Excuse me, sir, it's time to take the tray upstairs." He spun around and stared at her as though she'd spoken to him in Yoruba. "Your aunt's breakfast…"

"My wife's indisposed. You'll have to manage." His voice was strangled, as though whatever worried him held him firmly by the throat. He turned his back and continued pacing.

Blanche made fresh toast and warmed the grits and eggs in the microwave. She hoisted the tray and headed up the back stairs. She paused outside Grace's door but heard nothing. She knocked on Emmeline's door and called out that she'd brought breakfast. She hesitated, half-expecting Grace to come out of her own room and take the tray to Emmeline herself. But Grace didn't appear and Emmeline didn't respond. Blanche shifted the tray to her left hip and opened the door.

She was surprised to see Emmeline standing in the middle of the floor staring over Blanche's shoulder as though expecting someone else to enter as well. Her frown eased and she loosened her grip on the front of her robe when it was clear Blanche was alone. She nearly pounced on the tray Blanche set on the table.

"How're you today, ma'am?" Blanche reached for the over-flowing ashtray.

"Leave it," Emmeline told her in a voice that sounded like two large stones grinding against each other. "Bring me more eggs and some sausages, too, and be quick about it!" Emmeline stuffed half a slice of toast into her mouth as she spoke. She gulped down the glass of orange juice and wiped her mouth on the back of her hand before swirling the grits and eggs together and lighting into them.

Blanche turned to leave the room. Emmeline's arm shot out. She grabbed the skirt of Blanche's uniform. Her scrawny hand reminded Blanche of chicken feet. "Where is *she*?" Emmeline glared up at Blanche, still holding on to her uniform.

Blanche thought of pretending she didn't know who Emmeline was talking about, but there was a glint in the old lady's eye that stopped her. She don't look in the mood for no bullshit.

"She's indisposed. In her room, I guess."

"I'll just bet she's indisposed." Emmeline squinted up at Blanche with red-rimmed eyes. "Where's Everett?"

"In the living room. Acting like he got something on his mind." With utter nonchalance, Blanche twitched her skirt out of Emmeline's grasp. Their eyes met. Unlike her earlier eye-contact episode with Grace, it didn't even occur to Blanche to look away. She wasn't in the mood for any bullshit, either.

"Don't forget your place, gal!" Emmeline reached out and gave Blanche's skirt a sharp but brief tug. "Never mind the eggs and sausages. Bring me what's cooked and bring it now! And don't tell anyone. You hear me, gal? And make it fast!"

Blanche leaned down and slowly smoothed out the real and imaginary creases Emmeline had made in her uniform. Once again, she stared into Emmeline's eyes until the older woman turned her head away.

Every damned body in this house is nuts! Pulling on my clothes like I'm her property! In the kitchen she made herself a cup of tea and had a leisurely sit-down before she started the sandwiches. She enjoyed contradicting Emmeline's order to hurry as much as she enjoyed the tea.

The two ham sandwiches she finally carried upstairs were at least two inches thick. Yet, by the time Blanche had emptied the ashtrays, rinsed out Emmeline's liquor glass, and made the bed, both sandwiches had disappeared. Blanche thought about the hardly touched trays returned to the kitchen. Had Emmeline been pretending to be frail? What reason could she have had for hiding her hunger?

"How come you're so hungry?" The words were out of Blanche's mouth before she could stop them.

"None of your damned business." Emmeline reached for a cigarette. "And don't open your mouth about it to anyone. You hear me? Now get!"

Blanche stood outside the door for a few moments, fighting the urge to go back into that room and tell Emmeline what she could do to herself. It was a sweet thought, but there was nothing she could do without putting herself in jeopardy. She took a couple of deep breaths to calm herself. She hadn't forgotten her other reasons for wanting to come upstairs.

NINE

Blanche eased the guest room door open, quickly slipped inside, and closed the door behind her. She knew she was taking a risk. She'd already been told not to bother about this room, but she was sure she could handle Grace with a tale about hearing a noise or something.

The clothes were hanging in the closet, just as Mumsfield had said. And she'd been right about the shoes: Enna Jettick basic tie-up oxfords in shiny black leather. A dark green linen dress and black cardigan, and a set of used, clean, and expensive underwear of the non-sexy variety completed the outfit. She was immediately reminded of Uncle Will's forbidden Piedmont cigarettes hidden in the tool shed, just waiting for Aunt Mary to go to church so Uncle Will could go out to the shed and light up. These clothes had that same air of waiting at the ready. It can't be that, she whispered, it's too ridiculous. But what else could it mean? She'd seen it happen with other alcoholics she'd worked around. No matter how much booze they had at home, there were some drinkers who just had to be among their own, just like some people couldn't pray without going to church. And Emmeline was suddenly up and around and demanding more food. Logical behavior for someone gearing up to take a hike, although Blanche couldn't imagine where she expected to find drinking company out here in the country.

As she turned to leave the room, she realized there was something disturbed about the room, for one that got so little use. It felt full of secrets and comings and goings. She looked slowly around at the high old bed, the sheet-covered chairs, the heavy chest of drawers. One of the drawers wasn't quite closed. She pulled it toward her. It seemed abnormally heavy, until she saw the contents: five fifths of Seagram's gin snuggled in a green blanket like eggs in a nest. Close enough for Emmeline to fetch them herself. She left the guest room and went down the hall to Everett's room.

For a moment, she just stood before his closet with her arms folded across her chest. Her hopeful self told her that maybe Nate was mistaken. Some other man owned the pink jacket. She heaved a huge sigh and slid the closet door open.

It was actually more peach-colored, or salmon, much softer and more subtle than the cotton-candy color she'd been picturing. But to someone with no interest in the finer points of color, it was definitely a pink jacket. Like the azalea blossoms the night before, the jacket seemed to glow among the grays and tans that surrounded it. She stepped closer and reached for the right sleeve. It had creases around the lower part, where the sleeve had been rolled back. The left sleeve was the same. There was a small, stiff, dark red stain on the pale, satiny lining. One of the buttons had been pulled off with enough force to rip the fabric. She was struck by his arrogance, by the utter lack of concern that made it possible for him to keep a piece of evidence that could probably convict him. She searched the pockets. She told herself it was a waste of time and an unnecessary risk. What did she expect to find? The sheriff's badge? And what would she say if Everett walked in?

The jacket smelled faintly of a heavy, musty, very un-Grace-like perfume. She wondered if he'd had two reasons to go out last night. She shuddered at the idea of being made love to by a man with murder on his mind. There were bits of grit and gravel in the right-hand outside pocket. In the breast pocket her fingers touched something small, smooth, and cool. She held it up before her eyes with two fingers, careful not to drop it. It was a silver earring fastener for a pierced earring, the oblong kind with a hole through the middle. She looked at it, then put it back. She would have to pay particular attention the next time she saw Grace, but Blanche was already certain that Grace's ears weren't pierced. Not only is the man dangerous, she thought, he's careless. It might be that the only reason Grace didn't know about his affair was because she didn't want to know.

The phone was ringing when she reached the kitchen. "How about that sheriff bein' nice enough to put himself out of our misery?" Ardell said when Blanche picked up the receiver. "But before we get off on that subject, I got something serious to tell you, girl!" she added with some urgency. "I just come from Miz Minnie's. She told me she saw your mama and gave her some news for you. But Miz Minnie didn't tell her everything 'cause she didn't want Miz Cora to worry. You got to get out of there, girl!" Ardell sounded short of breath, as though she'd been running to get to the phone to call Blanche.

Blanche leaned so heavily against the kitchen counter, she could feel it cutting into her butt. Something in Ardell's voice told her she was going to need some support.

"That Everett was married to a woman named Jeannette first. But she died. Suicide. Least that's what they said in the papers and all. But you know the police don't press that crowd too hard. Miz Minnie said there was a lot of gossip about it in Atlanta, where it all happened. Some people said Jeannette and Everett weren't getting along too good, that he was running around on her, and that she was talking about divorcing him. She was the one with the money, so you know he didn't want to hear nothin' about no divorce!"

"How'd she die?" Blanche didn't like the tinny, tiny sound of her own voice, like a little kid afraid of the dark.

"She went out the window of the Central Plaza Hotel in Atlanta."

"What was she doing there?"

"Nobody knows. The room was rented in a made-up name."

Blanche suddenly longed for Everett not to be responsible for the death Ardell was telling her about, or for the one of which she herself suspected him. The more clear-cut his guilt, the more certain her own danger. She found herself arguing with Ardell, trying to make her news less awful.

"She could have rented the room because she wanted to jump out the window," she told Ardell.

"Sure. But why register under a phony name? And there was no note."

"Just because he mighta married the woman for her money don't necessarily mean he killed her. Maybe his stuff was so good it made her think she could fly!"

"This ain't no time for jokes, girl! We got to get you outta there!" Ardell scolded, then softened a bit. "But maybe you're right about the girlfriend. He had an alibi for the time she died. An alibi some folks said proved his story. Like it was impossible for him to be going with two women at once!"

"What kind of alibi? You mean Grace? She was with him when...Do you think she knows? Do you think she..." Blanche didn't want to finish the sentence, didn't want to contemplate the possibility of being in the house with two murderers. She lowered herself onto a chair.

"Seems like she don't want to know," Ardell said. "Folks down in Atlanta felt sorry for Grace for being so in love with Everett that she can't see him for what he is." Ardell paused for a moment.

"Well, she may be dumb and he may be a murderer, but at least the whole family ain't bad," she told Blanche. "There's that lawyer cousin, Archibald Symington. The old lady didn't speak to him for years 'cause he was in the civil rights movement. He's the lawyer who tried the sheriff of Jefferson County for Klan activity back in the late sixties."

Blanche was not impressed. "Yeah, but that was nearly thirty years ago. Now he's in the kiss-Emmeline's-ass movement from what I can see."

"So, what you gonna do, girlfriend?" Worry put a rasp in Ardell's voice. "Like I said, I could get a car and pick you up."

Blanche hesitated a moment. "It ain't that simple, Ardell." Blanche told her about the sheriff and Everett on the porch, about Everett going out in the limousine on the night the sheriff died, and about what Nate had had to say about it all. "How's it going to look if I walk outta here and they decide to call the police, say I stole something, maybe even claim the sheriff came out here to get me and that's the last time they saw him alive?"

"Oh, shit!" Ardell said.

"I'm not going to lose my head and do something stupid." Blanche's announcement was addressed to herself as well as to Ardell.

"I can't fault your reasoning, but I sure wish you'd just get the hell out of there."

"If I don't call you day after tomorrow, you call me," Blanche told her friend. "And if someone else answers the phone, tell 'em you got to talk to me. Tell 'em it's an emergency. If you see my kids, give 'em a kiss for me. And Mama, too. Bye."

Blanche continued to lean against the counter. Echoes of phrases from her conversation with Ardell bounced off the walls of her brain. I could die for this, she thought before she could stop herself. She knew it was stupid to scare herself, but she knew of too many innocent black people who'd gone to jail and never got out not to be afraid. "Criminal justice" was a term she found more apt than it was meant to be. She wondered whether Everett might be insane and decided all murderers were probably crazy, at least in the moment. But what about their supporters? Was the gossip that had gone around Atlanta about Grace true? Was she really so starry-eyed about Everett? How could she be? While Blanche couldn't answer all of her questions, she had some ideas about the last one. She'd participated in her share of relationships in which the main characters were the man she imagined her lover to be and herself. The actual man she was seeing was just the frame onto which she fitted the image of her dream man. And what a jolt it was to wake up one morning to find some sweating, needy, frightened flesh-and-blood man who acted as though he had some claim on her. In addition to the made-up-lover syndrome, which Blanche knew crossed class and color lines, Grace had grown up in the upper-class South during a time when there was no doubt pressure to produce a husband, even a tainted one.

But was she still starry-eyed enough to miss what Everett's taking a mistress might mean to her, given what had happened to his last wife? Grace also didn't act like a woman with that kind of jones for a man. Blanche decided she needed a cup of tea to mull it over.

She carried the kettle to the sink and reached for the cold-water tap. A prickly feeling along her arms made her set the kettle in the sink and wheel around. Everett was staring at her through the glass in the top of the back door. She clutched the sink behind her with both hands and made herself stand still, even though her whole body was screaming for her to run.

For a long moment, he stood with his hands cupping his eyes and his nose nearly touching the glass. He just stood there, looking at her with eyes she could see but couldn't read.

When Everett finally opened the door and entered the kitchen, Blanche told her shoulders to relax, her arms and hands to give up their tension, so that she could let go of the sink. But the blood, muscle, and what-all her arms and hands were made of didn't pay any attention to her orders. She continued clasping the sink as though it were her last hold on safety.

He looks a lot bigger out here, she thought. She nodded and relaxed her face into some semblance of pleasantness, trying to look like she wasn't so scared that she was about to lose control of her bladder. "Is there something I can get you, sir?"

Everett looked around the kitchen as if searching for something he could request. "I'd like a glass of water, please."

Blanche was grateful for a task that forced her to release the sink—if she had to run, she sure as hell couldn't drag the sink along. Getting the water also provided her with a weapon. She poured water from the refrigerator bottle into a water glass, dropped two ice cubes into it, and held it out to him with her left hand. She held the tray of ice cubes in her right hand. It wasn't much, but if he tried to grab her wrist, she intended to use the tray to break his nose.

Everett took the glass of water and thanked her. He took little sips from the glass instead of drinking it right down. The whole time, he watched Blanche. When he'd finished with the water, he handed her the glass and turned toward the back door. "Oh," he said, his hand just touching the doorknob. "Have you seen Nate?" He turned his head and looked at her over his shoulder.

Blanche hesitated for no more than half a second. "Not lately."

"But he was here earlier." He wasn't asking her, he was telling her. Blanche said nothing. "Didn't you two have a nice chat this morning?"

Everett's lips were stretched back and up into something totally unrelated to a real smile. She didn't try to return it. "Nate came in for a glass of water, sir. Just like you."

Everett was still looking over his shoulder at her. Now he turned to face her. His movements reminded her of creatures who crawled low to the ground and struck quick as lightning. In her mind, she navigated the route to the front door and the highway. "Anything else, sir?"

"Oh, yes! I nearly forgot," Everett told her in a voice that didn't speak of forgetfulness. "Mumsfield and I are off to the barber. We'll have something in town. Or later. My wife has a migraine. She's taken a sedative. I've looked in on my aunt. She's a bit sulky. Best left alone. You understand. She won't be wanting lunch, either." He stretched his lips at her once again. "When you see Nate, tell him I want to talk to him." He eased open the back door.

Blanche didn't answer and didn't move until she saw him walking down the backyard path toward the potting shed. She crossed her fingers and hoped Nate wasn't inside. The thought of Everett alone with Nate in that small, dark shed made her more than uneasy. But Everett only stuck his head in, then walked around the house toward the front drive. Blanche did a dance step to the bathroom when she heard the limousine drive off but sobered once she'd relieved herself. Ardell is exactly right, she thought. This is no time for fooling around. Blanche didn't doubt that Everett had it in him to either kill her or turn her in. Or both. And he'd certainly want her dead if he knew what she'd seen. She went back to the laundry room, unloaded the sheets from the washer, and folded them. When she was through, she wheeled the vacuum cleaner, duster, spray cleaner, and sponge into the living room. She parked her tools in the middle of the floor and chose a chair facing the stairs in case Grace wasn't as indisposed as Everett had said.

Blanche wondered if Everett had attacked her in the kitchen could she have struck back as she'd planned? Or was she so programmed to be somebody's victim that she couldn't break free to save her own life? The phone rang before she had time to think about her question. She hurried to the kitchen and grabbed it on the third ring. She listened before she spoke in case Grace picked up the phone elsewhere. "Hello? Hello? Is this five-two-zero-nine-four-nine?"

Blanche noticed that Mama was using her most proper tone. Her voice grew warmer and louder when she realized she'd reached Blanche. After she'd answered Blanche's questions about the health, well-being, and whereabouts of the children, she repeated what she'd learned from Miz Minnie about the household.

"You ain't got to worry 'bout the regular help coming back and interrupting anything. They gone down the coast, to Topsail. Go there every year. Ain't got no phone. Wouldn't talk to the likes of us no way. Live out Mount Airy. Hincty, I hear. Not Baptists. But never mind them. It's that old madame who's a sly, worldly fox."

"Emmeline? What about her?" The story her mother told surprised Blanche.

"Are you sure, Mama?" Blanche interrupted at one point. "This old party ain't sober enough to know a seed from a sow, half the time, let alone make a killing on the stock market. How much money? Damn! Excuse me, Mama, but that is a heavy heap of money. No wonder Everett and Grace were so willing to come live with Emmeline."

Still, the idea of Emmeline making big bucks on the stock market was so farfetched that Blanche wondered if perhaps Miz Minnie wasn't beyond her information-gathering prime. "Maybe Miz Minnie misunderstood."

Miz Cora laughed. "Girl," she told Blanche, "trying to hide from the truth is like trying to be invisible. You're right to be worried about yourself, but that don't change what is."

"And you better stay put for a while," her mother added. "This ain't the time to call attention to yourself by walking off the job."

"Yes, Mama...Yes, I am being careful."

And then the children were on the phone, reinforcing all her mother's admonitions to be careful. Taifa and Malik couldn't afford to lose another mother. Blanche listened for the resentment, fear, and distrust that went with feeling abandoned. She found enough warmth and trust and humor to reassure her that they were not feeling rejected. When she got off the phone, Blanche resumed her seat in the living room.

Funny how nothing is ever what it seems to be, she thought. To her, Emmeline was just a mean old drunk. She certainly didn't fit Blanche's image of a financial wizard. Yet, Mama claimed Emmeline had parlayed fifty thousand dollars of the money her husband had left her into thirty-five million dollars on the stock market. Miz Rachel, who did sewing for Emmeline, had been in

Emmeline's room pinning up a hem while Emmeline was taunting Everett with how much she was worth, how she had gotten it, and how little of it he had any hopes of ever touching.

Blanche looked around. The room was nice enough, but compared to some of the houses she'd worked in on Long Island, this was nowhere near multimillionaire quality. Then she remembered the Jamisons, for whom she'd worked when she first moved to New York. Harold and Christine Jamison had lived in an apartment not much better than the one in which Blanche had been living. But one day, she'd found a statement from their accountant in the trash. The Jamisons had enough money to buy their building and a few others besides. She'd immediately asked for a raise. Now she got up from her chair, plumped some cushions, picked a few pieces of lint off the carpet, and whipped her feather duster around the room. It was time to start dinner.

When the Rock Cornish game hens, complete with cornbread dressing, the braised leeks, the stuffed tomatoes, and the crusty rolls were arrayed in the dining room, Blanche went in search of the family. Grace had emerged from being indisposed and was sitting in the living room, not reading, not even looking out the window, just sitting with a listening look on her face, as though waiting for the other shoe to drop. Mumsfield was in the driveway with his head of freshly cut hair in the limousine's innards. Everett snatched his bedroom door open when Blanche tapped on it, and seemed relieved that it was only dinner Blanche had come to announce.

At dinner, Everett was in a state of high chatter, as though he'd been hired to make sure that no silences seeped into the room. His voice jabbed at Blanche as she served the food. Grace watched Everett, and nodded as he went on with his story about the time he and Bill Whoever were on the golf course and it began to rain and...Everett's voice had a chuckle in it, cuing them that at some point they were expected to be amused. Mumsfield looked from one to the other as though he were watching a tennis match, but he didn't halt his eating to listen.

Back in the kitchen, the first bit of cool evening breeze made the curtains dance. The birds lowered their voices in preparation to giving the airwaves over to creatures who made music with their hind legs. On Blanche's street, the children would be racing wildly up and down, screaming at the top of their lungs, made frantic by impending bedtime. She herself would have been ironing a skirt for tomorrow, or maybe reading the newspaper, or wondering whether she could save enough money to go to Greensboro to see Patti LaBelle next month—just being her own self in her own house, firmly attached to the people, places, and things that made up the thick cable which attached her to what she knew as her life, a life that didn't include living under the same roof with someone who had killed once and would undoubtedly kill her if he felt it would benefit him in any way. She tucked a sprig of parsley beside the Cornish hen on Emmeline's tray and felt herself unmoored in a way she'd never experienced before and hoped evermore to avoid.

When Grace came to fetch Emmeline's dinner, Blanche was just filling a small pitcher with iced tea, heavy on the sugar and tangy with lemon. Grace complimented her on "the fine dinner," picked up the tray, and left. It seemed to Blanche that she was hardly gone before she was back with the tray. The food was hardly touched. "She don't have much appetite, does she?" Blanche said, as she took the tray from Grace.

"She'd old and finicky," Grace told her. "It hasn't anything to do with your cooking," she added.

Blanche emptied the contents of Emmeline's tray into the garbage disposal and glanced at Grace. "She was hungry enough at lunch."

Grace didn't respond. She reminded Blanche of a childhood game in which someone spun you around by your arm and released you to hold the pose you fell into. Grace was standing as though the force of her spin had pried open her mouth and left it slightly ajar. Her head was tilted to the left. Her legs were spread and her upper body thrust forward. But while she looked somewhat dopey, her voice was sharp as glass shards when she finally did speak. Her eyes pinned Blanche's with an intense stare.

"What did she say? What did she tell you?" Grace's pose was broken now. She moved slowly toward Blanche, her eyes never leaving Blanche's face.

"She just seemed extra-hungry." Blanche fervently wished she'd kept her mouth shut. She moved away from Grace and put the salt and pepper shakers from Emmeline's tray in the cabinet by the sink.

"What did she say to make you think she was hungry?"

"It wasn't what she said, ma'am. She just seemed real eager for her lunch....Course, it coulda been my imagination, since I don't usually take her meals."

Grace continued to search Blanche's face. "Did she...did she ask for anything in particular to eat...or drink?"

So that's it, Blanche thought. "No, ma'am," she told Grace in a slow drawl meant to convey her lack of concern about the conversation, as evidenced by her lack of memory on the subject. "She didn't hardly say anything at all, that I recall."

Blanche turned to the sink, and began running water to wash Emmeline's plate and glass. Tension was rising in the room like heat. Behind her, Grace suddenly folded into a kitchen chair with a thump. She began speaking in a low, rapid voice. "Of course, it wouldn't have happened if I'd been well, if I'd taken her tray up as I ought to have done. It's really my fault. But it's so difficult. So hard. You can't imagine.

"No one knows, of course," she went on. "Not even Mumsfield. We've managed to keep it from him, somehow. If only she would stop, or at least cut down. Now she's up there snoring and drooling and..."

Unlike the last time Grace had attempted to confide in her, Blanche was as interested in getting into Grace's business as

Grace seemed to be in telling it. She was tempted to launch into a full-fledged lay-it-on-my-bosom number, complete with wet eyes and hand-patting, but that role was too familiar for a Mistress of the Manor type like Grace. Instead Blanche let her arms fall to her sides and was attentively silent. Her head slightly bowed, she waited for her employer to bestow the privilege of confidence.

"Are you married, Blanche?"

Blanche raised her head. "Yes, ma'am," she lied.

"Any children?"

"No, ma'am." She didn't want even the knowledge of her kids in this house. "That man is more than enough child for me." She gave Grace a version of that pained, puzzled, and indignant look which is part of all women's male vocabulary.

Grace sighed, propped her elbows on the table, and rested her head on her hands, as though she couldn't bear the weight of her own thoughts.

"He's not really insensitive, you know." She raised her head and looked at Blanche. "He's really quite kind, quite caring. It's just that he doesn't understand how difficult it is. She's not an easy person." She sighed deeply. "But then, neither is Everett, some-times…But Aunt Emmeline is wrong about him. He wouldn't!" Grace jumped as though she'd been pinched.

"What did your aunt say?" Blanche kept her voice as neutral as possible.

Grace stood up. "I'm talking too much." She put a fist on either side of her head, as though to keep its halves in place. "And my head is splitting." She hurried out of the room.

Blanche slumped against the sink. She was conscious of the dampness under her arms and in her crotch. She chided herself for having frightened Grace off. She'd known her question was a risk, but she thought Grace was close enough to hysteria to be prompted. Too bad. But she'd be back. Blanche was sure of it. She tried to imagine what Emmeline could have told Grace about Everett and how she could possibly know anything, sitting up there drunk in her room. For a moment, Blanche let herself feel what it must be like to be Grace right now, knowing, or at least suspecting, that her husband was a murderer. Not only was he a killer, but she had lousy taste in men. But from what Ardell had said, maybe Grace had married him knowing he was a murderer. Her lips curled into a wry smile at the idea that Grace was a woman who believed she could change a man by marrying him taken to the extreme. She finished washing Emmeline's dishes and put the tray away.

She wanted to go to bed. She was as tired as if she'd been doing stoop labor all day. But she was chock-full of other people, too, as though Emmeline, Mumsfield, Everett, and Grace had taken possession of her person, with their commands, needs, questions, and fears. She would likely choke on them if she lay down. She opened the back door and stepped outside. Immediately she was wrapped in an eastern Carolina night, moist and gentle, loud with creatures' songs and the whisper of the pines. Blanche sunk down on the doorstep and released her unwelcome inhabitants in a series of deep, slow sighs. She rose, went back in the kitchen, and turned the lights off. Back outside, she let her Night Girl self slip down the yard to walk slowly between the two halves of the vegetable garden, carrots and corn on one side, tomatoes and peas on the other. The cabbage leaves were delicate fans quivering on the bit of breeze that kept the night from being muggy. She felt the darkness drifting down from the sky, passing through her pores, into her bloodstream, her bones, and her heart. She breathed deeply, hastening the night's penetration. She smiled at the return of the childhood Night Girl feeling that she could leap as high as the housetops, if she chose, or even ride the stars, as Cousin Murphy had said.

In this state, her brain was suddenly cleared of all the little bits of worry and commentary that interfered with her ability to latch on to a thought. She stood away from herself and looked at where she was. My whole life could depend on what happens in this house, she thought. She turned to look at the house behind her. It seemed to Blanche to have a kind of worried air, as though it knew that murder had been done by one of its inhabitants. She knew who the murderer was and had some idea of why he'd killed. She could see that this knowledge was dangerous to her, even though no one else seemed to think the sheriff had been murdered. Except Nate. She wondered why he hadn't come back to finish their conversation.

Maybe he's gone to the police, she thought in the part of herself that was prone to pessimism and panic. But her mind was still filled with the night, which brooked no nonsense. Nate hadn't lived to be an old black man by going to the police and accusing high-toned white men of murder.

"Nate," she whispered softly. She laid her open hand on the door of the potting shed. Her fingers, the wood, and the night formed a pattern in shades of darkness. She turned and walked back to the stoop and sat down. I'll wait a bit, she decided. He might still drop by.

TEN

She might have slept on the back stoop all night if a mosquito with a stinger as thick as a broom handle hadn't attacked her elbow. She shuffled off to bed to save her skin.

She woke to the memory of a noise in the night. Loud. High-pitched. A train whistle? Car brakes? A scream? She flung back the sheet and the thin blue blanket and planted her feet firmly on the chilly linoleum.

Something had changed. She could feel it the moment she stepped outside her bedroom door. At first, she thought the house had been broken into and its privacy shattered. But she saw nothing out of place as she tiptoed down the second-floor hall. She listened at all the bedroom doors and heard nothing, and nothing looked amiss. Yet, something had happened. When she'd first arrived, the house had had a timid kind of feeling, like a dog who'd been kicked too many times. When she'd looked at the house from out back last night, it had seemed worried. Now the house seemed to have somehow divorced itself from the household as surely as if a lawyer had served papers.

"What is it, Blanche?" Mumsfield was waiting in the kitchen, sitting very still, his hands folded on the edge of the table.

"I don't know, Mumsfield, honey." She wasn't at all surprised that he should feel it, too.

She crossed the room and turned on the green plastic radio on the windowsill. She drummed her fingers on the counter and shifted from foot to foot while some good ole boy invited everybody to come on down and be rooked at his used-car lot, and a

woman with a husky voice tried to sell seaside condos by imply-
ing they came with a year's supply of pussy. Blanche reached for
a knife and began halving oranges for juice. The station segued
into national news. It was after the national news that a young
man trying to suppress his Southern accent told her that the
noise she'd heard in the night was a fire engine on its way to "the
fatal fire at the cabin of Nate Taylor, near Oman's Bluff—the site
of another tragic death recently."

Mumsfield began softly sobbing into his cupped hands. His
body rocked slowly from side to side. Blanche remained dry-
eyed, although her body was momentarily doused in pain, as
Nate's must have been until the flames ate him.

She turned off the radio when the reporter moved on to talk
about the mayor's meeting with representatives of the Beautify
Our City Committee. For a second, she let herself pretend that
it was some other Nate, near some other Oman's Bluff. It was
just too damned much! It wasn't enough that the man had been
treated like a machine, robbed of respect, and kept poor all of
his life. It wasn't enough that his time had been owned by other
people who also decided how high he could raise his eyes and his
voice, and where he could live and how. He also had to be murdered over some white people's shit that didn't have a damned
thing to do with him.

A thick, hot rage began to roil in her stomach at the thought
of the deaths of all the poor black Nates and, yes, Blanches at the
hands of the privileged white Everetts of the world. Nowadays,
people wanted to tell you class didn't exist and color didn't matter anymore. Look at Miss America and the chairman of the
Joint Chiefs of Staff. But Miss America and the chairman were
no more black people than Mother Teresa was white people. Men
like Nate and women like her were the people, the folks, the mud
from which the rest were made. It was their hands and blood
and sweat that had built everything, from the North Carolina
governor's mansion to the first stoplight. They ought to have

been appreciated for being the wattle that held the walls together. Instead, they were expendable, interchangeable, rarely missed, hardly regarded, easily forgotten. Not this time! There was no question in her mind that Everett had killed Nate, no matter what they said on the radio.

Why hadn't she expected this to happen? Or had she? If she'd acted on last night's concern for Nate's whereabouts, instead of hanging around the back stoop hoping he'd show up, maybe he'd still be alive. I could've tried to find his place last night, or looked for him earlier, she told herself. If she'd found him and added what she suspected to what he already knew, she was sure he'd have understood the danger and gone away for a while, as black people in the South have always been forced to do when they come to the attention of the wrong white person. Tears gathered as she pictured Nate off somewhere safe, making himself a new garden that was all his own. Her tears made dark blotches on the front of her gray uniform.

"Don't cry, Blanche. Don't cry." Mumsfield's voice was choked by his own tears. He knelt in front of her, reached out, hesitated, then awkwardly patted her hand.

"Everyone has to die, Blanche."

Blanche smiled a wry smile. He was a good pupil. But the fact that we've all got to die sure as hell don't give nobody the right to kill you, she thought. She patted Mumsfield's hand, each of them now trying to comfort the other.

The man on the radio had said the fire department suspected Nate of falling asleep while smoking. Blanche was very sensitive to smoke. When she'd been with Nate, she'd never picked up even a whiff of the telltale odor all smokers carry in their clothes and hair.

Only a crazy person keeps killing people and killing people, she thought, and realized she had no reason to think Everett wasn't crazy. He was a rich white male. Being in possession of that particular set of characteristics meant a person could do pretty much anything he wanted to do, to pretty much anybody he chose—like an untrained dog chewing and shitting all over the place. Blanche was sure having all that power made many men crazy. And, according to Ardell, Everett had already exercised his privilege in the most lethal of ways once before. She thought about yesterday, when Everett had questioned her about her conversation with Nate. Everett had sniffed around her answers like a hunting dog with the scent of possum in its nose.

"I need to get away from here!"

"No, Blanche! No! Please don't leave, Blanche, please." Mumsfield gripped her hand.

Blanche gave him a sad smile. It was too bad he was related to these people, too bad he wasn't black or at least on her side of the household. Too bad she couldn't tell him that despite her outburst, he needn't worry about her leaving—not until she saw to it that something awful happened to his cousin Everett.

"I better start breakfast."

"You won't leave Mumsfield, will you, Blanche?"

"Not without telling you, Mumsfield, honey." She hoped she was telling the truth. She took her hand back and rose from the chair.

While she cooked, Mumsfield sat watching her move from refrigerator to sink to stove and back again. Ordinarily, having someone hanging around the kitchen watching her cook would have irritated her. Today, there was comfort in their shared grief. It was likely to be the last time she would talk with him and be with him just drylongso. He was a member of Everett's family. She would have to treat him as someone with more interest in saving Everett than in avenging Nate's murder. She felt very alone but not saddened by it. The fiery rage in her belly and the ice encasing her heart made her unfit for human companionship. Only Everett's long and miserable imprisonment or his death could return her to normal. "He will not get away with this," she mouthed soundlessly while swirling butter in a sauté pan. "He will not!"

Mumsfield helped her set the table. While she finished the eggs, he carried the tray of grapefruit halves and orange juice into the dining room, then went to fetch Everett and Grace.

Everett entered the dining room first. His back was so stiff it might have been in a brace. Grace followed him. Her eyes were riveted on the back of his head. The two of them seemed to move in tandem, caught at opposite ends of a taut rubber band that twanged with tension.

Blanche arranged the food on the sideboard. She pushed away the fantasy of dashing the food, and everything else she could lay her hands on, into Everett's smug face—scalding coffee, thick, stick-to-the-skin grits. She took a deep breath, relaxed her shoulders, and listened for what would be said once Mumsfield blurted out what he'd just heard on the kitchen radio. But Mumsfield was silent. Blanche looked over her shoulder. He had launched into his grapefruit with the same single-mindedness he brought to all other tasks. A time to mourn and a time to eat breakfast, she thought, and recognized the naturalness of Mumsfield's world, in which mourning had nothing to do with eating. The body didn't stop needing nourishment because the heart was broken; the living had to live. It was a philosophy she was sure Nate would have appreciated. She readied herself for closer contact with Everett.

She removed the fruit plates from the table, then served the eggs, bacon, hash browns, and grits.

Grace waved away the food without shifting her gaze from Everett. Her face was pale, her eyes were red and wide. She's like a TV set that can only get one channel, Blanche thought. She wondered what would happen to Grace if that station went silent or, like now, simply refused to broadcast on her frequency.

Everett continued to act as though nothing and no one existed beyond his newspaper, just as he'd done the morning after the sheriff was murdered. Blanche was on full alert as she moved closer to him, but she wasn't prepared for the sudden wave of revulsion that made her skin turn cold when their hands accidentally touched. Everett took a teaspoonful of eggs and a slice of bacon, which he promptly ignored. Mumsfield had his usual sizable helping of each dish.

When she leaned over Everett to fill his coffee cup, a slight tremor ruffled the newspaper. Everett quickly laid it down and glanced up at her as if to see if she'd noticed. He's like a hostage, or a drowning man, she thought, in the moment that their eyes met. He smoothed back his already unruffled hair in a gesture that Blanche understood to be his brand of hand-wringing. She smiled at his discomfort. It eased the pain of serving him. Still, her face flushed with shame. She told herself she had no other choice than to act as she was. She accepted the truth of this, but somehow it wasn't enough to stop her from feeling as though she'd betrayed herself and Nate in some way. I'll bring him down, she told Nate, on her way back to the kitchen. Somehow or another, I'll make him pay. I promise.

She expected Mumsfield to come back to the kitchen when he finished his breakfast, but it was Grace who slipped by the swinging door. She stood by the table slowly wringing her hands.

"My husband and I will be out for lunch." She spoke quickly, as if she expected to be interrupted or told to shut up. "My aunt has had a restless night, and she's in a fierce mood. So if you'll prepare a thermos of soup and perhaps some sandwiches for her lunch, I'll take them up when I take up her breakfast tray. That way you needn't disturb her while we're out."

"Yes, ma'am." Blanche waited for Grace to leave. Grace blinked at her a few times.

"You've heard about it on the radio, haven't you?" Grace asked.

"Ma'am?"

"About Nate, about the fire....I wanted to come tell you before breakfast, as soon as I heard, but my husband said..."

Blanche didn't understand why she wanted to lie to Grace but decided to follow her first mind.

"What about Nate, ma'am?"

"He's dead."

"Oh, Lord!" Blanche lifted her apron to her face as she'd seen Butterfly McQueen do in *Gone With the Wind*. If the subject had been anything other than Nate's death, she'd have had a hard time keeping a straight face. It was the kind of put-on that gave her particular pleasure. But now she only wanted to appear convincingly simple. She rubbed her eyes to moisten and redden them, and raised her head to regard her enemy's helpmate.

"What happened, ma'am?" she asked. Her face felt hard and sharp, as though she'd used her apron to wipe away all of her softness.

"There was a fire. Last night. At his place. He must have been asleep." Grace's hands continued to wrestle with each other.

Blanche folded her arms across her chest. "It sure is a shame." She shook her head from side. "He seemed like a nice old man.... Was his wife..."

"Oh, no," Grace told her quickly. "He didn't have a wife, or other family. He was alone when he...when the house burned down."

Yes, of course, Blanche thought, the house burned down. Nobody burned it down. Nobody knocked Nate out or threw a lighted cigarette on his old newspapers and roasted him alive. The house burned down.

Grace continued talking. "Perhaps he was a very sound sleeper. Perhaps the roof collapsed before he could get to the door."

Blanche ducked her head and tugged at her apron until the tightness had drained out of her face and she'd blinked the scalding tears from her eyes.

"Too bad," Grace went on. "But, of course, you didn't really know him, did you?"

Blanche didn't bother to tell Grace that she had known Nate better and more truly in twenty-four hours than any rich white bitch could have known him in a lifetime. "Did he work for ya'll a long time?" she asked instead.

Grace's eyes widened. "Why, he's been here since I was a child." There was a wistful note in her voice.

"You used to come here as a little girl?" Blanche asked the question as though there were something deeply fascinating about this particular piece of Grace's history. It was really her need to change the subject that prompted the question. She didn't know how much of this woman's nonchalance about Nate's death she could take. Better to get her off on everybody's favorite subject.

Grace slipped into a chair and folded her arms on the table in front of her. "I was just five that first summer. I remember I wore a…" Grace's eyes filled with recollections. A bittersweet smile curled her thin lips as she talked of polka-dot sundresses and homemade ice cream. There was no mention of Nate in Grace's description of how the house and its inhabitants had looked to her little girl eyes. He was also forgotten in her tale of childhood summers spent romping through the wondrous woods around the house. The KKK story Nate had told was obviously not a landmark in the life of his savior.

While Grace rambled through her childhood, Blanche worked at getting her temper under control. She thought it unlikely that Grace knew the particulars of Nate and the sheriff's deaths, mostly because she couldn't imagine Everett telling Grace about them.

"…It was the third summer that I met Everett. He…"

Blanche responded to Everett's name. "It's like ya'll was meant to be married from birth, ain't it, ma'am?" Blanche used her tone of voice and her facial expression to say how romantic she found this idea.

"Oh, yes!" Grace leaped at the idea like a hungry cat at liver, just as Blanche knew she would. Blanche understood what a relief it was to find a soft, warm memory to distract the mind from the unpaid rent, the lost love, the sick child, the murdering husband. When Grace eventually stopped to take a breath, Blanche fine-tuned the course of the conversation. "It must be wonderful to be with the same man since childhood."

"Oh, yes!...I mean...We haven't been together all that time, exactly...He..."

Blanche chuckled. "Oh, I know how it is with a man! He sees someone different, someone younger or prettier, or..." Blanche left room for Grace to add "richer," in her mind, and then went on. "And off he goes, just like a puppy after a rabbit. Then here he comes back, tail between his legs, looking to be fed."

Grace didn't answer for so long, Blanche thought she'd made a mistake to use such a broad and obvious prompt.

"If only he trusted me more, talked to me!" She gave Blanche an anguished look. There was more warmth and feeling in her voice than Blanche had heard before. Spots of red dotted her cheeks and neck. "Whatever it is, I know I could help him. I know I could!" She raised her hands and opened her arms and fingers as though grasping an invisible Everett and pulling him to her chest. "I could arrange things so that...This family has connections!" she added, with a little toss of her head. Then she caught her breath and stared into middle space, a look of loss and pain on her face, as though confronted with some awful vision. She was quite still for few moments, after which she seemed to collapse in on herself. Her shoulders rounded, her hands fell heavily to her sides. Tears pooled in her eyes and began a slow course down to her chin.

"What's the use?" she mumbled. She shook her head slowly from side to side. "What's the use?" She rose, turned, stumbled to the swinging door, and pushed her way into the dining room.

Blanche was pleased. Grace might not know anything, but she clearly suspected something. Blanche opened a can of chicken rice soup and marveled at the sort of woman who thought she could make everything right for her man, even if she didn't know what "everything" was, just as she could change him from being a louse into a sweetheart. Despite her shortsightedness and romantic nonsense, Grace was not to be dismissed. She might turn out to be useful.

While the soup heated, Blanche cut the crusts from four slices of bread. Grace would never turn Everett over to the police. But she must know something that could be used to convince other people of Everett's guilt. Whatever it was, Blanche was prepared to pump Grace hard to get it. She sliced the meat from the leftover Cornish hens and softened some cream cheese. She would have to find a way to start another conversation with Grace. She turned off the fire under the simmering soup, found a thermos in the pantry, and filled it.

Blanche had a feeling the whole business with the soup and the sandwiches was for her benefit. She sliced a few olives and put them in the sandwiches, then covered the dish with a silver plate cover. She diced some ham for Emmeline's omelet, broke two eggs into a bowl, and seasoned them, while a pan heated. She thought it was terrible to waste so much food, but she had to play her part. She eased the omelet onto a warm plate.

"Is it ready yet?" Blanche jumped an inch off the floor at the sound of Everett's voice. A faint creak on the other side of the door to the dining room had told her somebody was headed for the kitchen, but she'd expected Grace. Everett was standing just inside the door. "I've come for the tray. Is it ready?"

"Almost." Blanche poured water over the tea leaves and thought about flinging the water in his face.

Everett smoothed his hair and frowned slightly as he looked out the window. Blanche set the tray on the table. She didn't trust herself to hand it to him.

"She's not well, you know," he said, without moving to take up the tray. "Not...not physically ill. Just...sometimes she imagines...She's under a good deal of strain. I hope she hasn't...Do you know what I mean?" he asked when Blanche made no reply.

"She's old," Blanche told him.

"No. I mean my wife."

For the first time since he'd entered the room, Blanche looked directly at him.

"I simply thought you should know," Everett said after a long pause. "In case she should say something..."

In case she should say something about you being a psycho, Blanche thought. And dragging out that tired crazy-woman number! She wished she had a nickel for every time some man had told her she was nuts, just at the moment in their relationship when she was letting him know that she saw him for what he was.

The silence between them began to crackle. "I'll take that now." Everett snatched the tray from the table and quickly backed through the swinging door to the dining room.

Once he'd gone, she realized she hadn't been frightened of him. Wary, yes, and ready to scream and run, but not afraid. Probably because there was no sense in both of us being scared, she thought. She was sure it was fear she'd felt wafting off him like mist from a frozen lake. Not of her, but of something, someone. Maybe he really thought Grace was about to crack. That pleased her. If he was afraid, he was that much closer to doing something stupid, perhaps something even money and influence couldn't cover up—although she was hard pressed to imagine what this could be. Still, if he'd been his usual arrogant self, he'd never have made that little speech about Grace. Blanche hummed as she cleared away the breakfast dishes.

When Mumsfield did come to the kitchen, it wasn't Nate he had on his mind, at least not the first time. "Blanche! The car is dented. On the fender!" He pointed toward the driveway. He said "dented" as though it meant the same as "totaled."

"When did it happen, Blanche? When?" He started pacing around the kitchen.

"Hold it!" Blanche blocked his path. "None of that ripping and running in here! Sit down and tell me about it."

"A dent!" he told her again when he was seated, and in the same incredulous tone of voice.

"I take it you didn't hit anything."

"Never, Blanche! Never!"

"How long do you think it's been there, Mumsfield, honey?"

"Since today! This morning! There was no dent yesterday, Blanche." His eyebrows drew a straight line over his eyes.

"So who else could have done it?" she asked him with her voice in neutral.

Mumsfield's mouth formed a perfect circle. Blanche mentally supplied the "Oh" that went with it and wondered what had caused it. Surely Mumsfield wasn't thinking that Everett had used the car to go kill Nate, as she was. His next words made it clear what was on his mind.

"Cousin Everett crashed his own car," Mumsfield told her. His face was in a deep frown. Blanche thought she heard a shade of Nate's intonation when Mumsfield referred to Everett.

"You don't like him."

Mumsfield blushed, lowered his eyes, and began fiddling with his fingers.

"You don't have to like him, you know." She was tempted to tell him that she herself hated the man.

"But he's my cousin, Blanche. Aunt Em says…"

"Just like you don't have to like all of your relatives, you also don't have to agree with everything a person says because you love her."

"He laughs at me, too, Blanche."

It was Blanche's turn to form a wordless "Oh" and avert her eyes from the bittersweet amusement in his. There are no fools out here, she thought, only a whole lot of ways of getting to the same place.

Blanche was stuffing towels into the washing machine when Grace returned Emmeline's breakfast tray. Most of the food was gone. Down the toilet, Blanche thought. Grace said that she and Everett were leaving, that Mumsfield was somewhere about the place, and reminded Blanche not to disturb "poor Aunt Emmeline."

Blanche went through the house to a front window, where she watched the limousine slide down the drive. She could feel Mumsfield in the kitchen waiting for her. He was pacing, almost skipping, around the room. His eyes were bright.

"Mumsfield is going to get us something special, Blanche. Something we need!" he told her.

"And what might that be?"

Mumsfield grinned at her. "You'll see, Blanche, you'll see!"

"Well, you'll tell me when you're ready, I suppose."

"I'll show you, Blanche. I'll get it right now, right now!" The back door banged shut behind him.

Blanche hardly paid him any mind. Her attention was already upstairs.

The guest room closet, when she opened it, was as empty as she'd expected it to be. Now she stood outside Emmeline's door trying to decide what to do. What if she was wrong and the old lady was inside? She'd undoubtedly complain to Grace about Blanche's knocking on her door. Blanche grasped the cool porcelain knob with its old rose pattern and turned it slowly and firmly as far to the right as it would go and then all the way to the left. Locked. She hesitated a few more moments before Night Girl rescued her.

"Excuse me, ma'am." She knocked gently at the door. "I know you don't want to be bothered, but I keep smelling something like wood smoke out here in the hall and I was wondering if... Ma'am? Ma'am?" Blanche knocked harder, but she got no answer and expected none.

She was right. The old girl had run off, and Everett and Grace had gone out looking for her. They had to. Everett didn't want the cops snooping around here for any reason. And neither of them wanted Emmeline found drunk in some roadside joint.

Blanche was back in the kitchen when the phone rang. "It's me, gal. Don't pretend you don't know who this is." Emmeline's voice was badly slurred. It took Blanche a couple of seconds to figure out who she was. She held the receiver to her ear and waited.

"Now, you listen close. I want you to give Everett a message. Tell him I wrote a letter. It's got everything in it. Everything. I sent it to Archibald. I told him to open it if he don't hear from me by Friday. Tell him that!"

Blanche hung up the phone and put water in the kettle. When the water was ready, she made a pot of tea and settled down at the kitchen table to think. How could Emmeline have found out what Everett had done? Her windows looked out on the front of the house. Had she, too, seen Everett leaving the house the night of the sheriff's murder? Blanche squeezed a few drops of lemon into her tea. Whatever Emmeline knew, there was no reason for her to run off. She could simply have called Archibald and told him on the phone, or told him to come to see her here if she was frightened. There was a phone in her room. Was she brain damaged enough to pretend she'd written the letter as a way of forcing Everett to see that she got a couple of days of uninterrupted binging? It was a dangerous game to play. Even if there was a letter, having it read didn't mean Everett would be arrested and dragged off to jail.

Blanche remembered when the Holder boy had stabbed the fifteen-year-old son of a sharecropper on his granddaddy's place. The police had labeled it self-defense. The family lawyer—the man Blanche was working for at the time—had put the boy in a cushy psychiatric clinic for six months, until the publicity died down. Then the boy's mother had taken him off to ski in Switzerland and travel around Europe for a year. The newspapers implied that the sharecropper boy had made improper advances toward the Holder boy. Everyone who worked in the kitchens of the town knew it was likely to have been the other way round.

Blanche sipped her cooling tea and wondered if Everett thought his little speech had convinced her that Grace might make up stories about him, or whether he had other bits of evidence of Grace's insanity lined up. Maybe Blanche wasn't the only one who needed to be concerned about being framed. She tugged her panties into a more comfortable relationship to her crotch and carried her cup and the teapot to the sink. None of this thinking relieved her of her other tasks. She gathered her tools.

Since it was Wednesday, she went back upstairs to the linen closet and counted out clean sheets before going into Everett's room. The order she'd imposed on his room the day before had been buried beneath a fresh layer of discarded socks, shorts, and undershirts, damp towels, and shoes lying in the middle of the floor.

What am I looking for? she asked herself as she stirred the already jumbled contents of Everett's bureau drawers. She thought of looking around the room for something greatly out of place, but not much in this room seemed to have a place. The chair that had been by the window the last time she was in the room was now near the foot of the bed, in front of the blanket chest.

Blanche sat in the chair. She leaned forward and ran her finger along the ridge carved in the edge of the chest's lid. She didn't know what she expected to find inside, but what she found, beneath a blanket and a spare pillow, was a pair of handcuffs. She tried to picture Everett handcuffed to the bedposts while Grace gave him a good spanking, or vice versa. It didn't work either way. She turned the handcuffs over and over in her hands as if she expected their cool gray-blue metal to tell her whether or not they had belonged to the sheriff—or had been used in Nate's murder. Her hands felt suddenly cold, even though she was wearing rubber gloves. She quickly replaced the cuffs. It won't be long now, she told herself. Not long. She hurried through Everett's room and closed the door firmly behind her.

Before she changed the bed in Grace's room, she flipped through Grace's address book until she found an entry for Archibald. She used a sheet of Grace's monogrammed stationery to jot down his office and home numbers. She was careful to return the pen to exactly the spot where she'd found it. She gathered the sheets and carried them down to the laundry room. Maybe the best thing to do was to forget about the call and hope Archibald didn't hear from Emmeline on Friday. But what if the letter was a fake?

Mumsfield burst through the back door, his face tightly scrunched up in a grin. "Here it is, Blanche. This one is for you." He carefully placed a blue-green rock dusted with rusty soil on the kitchen table. "There!" Blanche was sure she could feel the warmth from the smile he gave her. "Now we have him for always, Blanche."

Blanche looked at the stone for a few minutes, then at Mumsfield. It was clear from his attitude that the rock was important, and she could see from the way he was beaming that he was pleased with himself for getting it and giving it to her. She cautioned herself to tread lightly. "Tell me about rocks," she said.

Mumsfield seemed to grow half an inch taller while she watched. "Sure, Blanche. I will tell you about rocks. I understand rocks," he told her. "Rocks have deep parts, Blanche. Nate told me." He was looking at the rock on the table as he spoke. "Rocks hold things. Deep inside. Forever. Rocks remember. Rocks from Nate's place have Nate inside." He picked up the rock and held it out to Blanche with both hands.

"Can't you feel Nate laughing, Blanche?" Mumsfield asked her once she'd taken the stone from him. "Can't you hear him, Blanche?" Mumsfield bent over, slapped his knee, and wagged his head from side to side in soundless imitation of Nate having a good laugh.

Lord! What a wonder this boy is, Blanche thought. She blinked back her tears and thanked him for bringing Nate back to her. She made a mat for the rock from a folded paper towel and set it on the windowsill. "Where he can watch the garden grow," she told Mumsfield.

They stood in front of the window for a minute or two, looking at the rock and the garden beyond. Earlier, Blanche had wondered about Nate's funeral and whether she'd be able to attend. Now she no longer cared about that ritual.

Mumsfield ended their memorial service with a question about the possibility of early lunch. Blanche cooked a pound of bacon and fixed him four of the world's largest bacon, lettuce, and tomato sandwiches. Mumsfield was just polishing them off with three glasses of milk when the delivery boy scratched at the back door. Mumsfield went upstairs to put on his red suspenders, then left to work on some truck or other at the garage down some road or other.

Blanche did the dishes and began sweeping the floor. Instead of dust or crumbs, each stroke of her broom seemed to stir up the chill that had settled in the house despite the warm day. It wasn't a welcoming cool that provides shelter from the heat, but a forlorn cold that made the sunny day feel washed out and working its way toward gray. She propped the broom against the refrigerator and called her kids. She spoke to her mother first.

"I talked to Miz Minnie just this morning," Blanche's mother said. "She told me that attorney minister man is kin to them folks you're with."

"Attorney who, Mama?"

"You know who I mean, girl! The one who's investigatin' the sheriff."

"The state attorney general?"

"That's right, him." Her tone congratulated Blanche on finally getting it right.

"He's kin to these folks?"

"Blanche, don't keep repeatin' everything I say like some kind of poll parrot! And don't go askin' me a lotta questions about him. 'Cause he ain't had nothin' to do with them since his only child drowned in they pond."

Blanche wondered if not talking to them included not taking their money. Of course, the attorney general might not be the person the sheriff had intended to bribe. If he was the person, he might not have known or cared where the sheriff was getting the money.

"Mama, ask Miz Minnie if the attorney general is in need of quick money."

"'Course he is! You know how white folks what got money is about gettin' more money."

"Well, ask her to find out if his need is any greater than usual, and if so, why."

"I sure will be glad when you're outta them folks' house!"

Blanche reminded her mother of the yet-to-be-received income-tax check that was the key to her getaway. But she didn't mention her other reason for not being ready to leave.

"Shame about that man out there. Must be terrible to burn up like that."

Blanche agreed but didn't elaborate. She was glad her mother didn't seem to want to dwell on it.

It was a few minutes after the children took over the phone before Blanche felt the warmth she'd been seeking when she called. To protect herself, she'd had to put the part of her that was connected to them behind a locked door in the back of her being, waiting for the time when she could be her full self again. Now she felt like a prisoner being allowed a moment of family. She had to stretch to reach across the gulf, to really be with them. She moaned with Taifa over having just missed winning first prize in the playground foot race. When Malik came on the line, she listened sympathetically and agreed—without undermining her mother's authority or condoning his occasional use of brute force—that his grandmother might not understand boys as well as she did girls.

When she hung up the phone, her goose bumps were gone, and while the house was no warmer, the cold didn't cut to her marrow. She dialed Ardell. "It's me, Ardell. How you doin', girl?" Blanche eased herself onto a kitchen chair.

"I heard about Nate. It's a damned shame," Ardell told her.

A few hours earlier, a remark like that would have sent Blanche into a firestorm of rage and tears. Now she calmly told Ardell what she thought had really happened.

"I'd like to see the fucker ten feet underground, myself," Ardell told her. "But he ain't no cream puff, girl. Sounds to me like the boy's 'bout as crazy as you can get without frothing at the mouth!"

Blanche had expected Ardell to be worried by her determination to nail Everett. "You know how you get when you're real mad, girlfriend. You don't want to say anything that will get you in more trouble than you can handle."

Blanche laughed. "Them diplomatic lessons you been takin' are paying off!"

"Well, you got to do what you got to do when you dealing with a prickly cactus, Blanche."

"All right. But you know I can't walk away from this."

And, of course, she did know. She also knew that the police were more likely to arrest Blanche than they were to even question Everett. As they talked, Blanche listened for the sound of the limousine and waited for the tingling of her scalp that would tell her someone was nearby.

"Do you think the letter is real?" Ardell asked when Blanche told her about Emmeline's threat. "Maybe she's just making it up so they'll let her party till Friday."

"But she must know something dangerous, or the threat wouldn't mean anything, would it? Maybe I should tell Grace. It might keep Everett from killing Emmeline." She didn't want anyone's blood but Everett's on her conscience.

"Miz Minnie says they're probably both deep in this," Ardell told her. "You know Coreen's brother Samuel? Well, he has an old lodge buddy who lives in Atlanta. The buddy's next-door neighbor was working for Grace's people when Everett's wife died. She says Grace told the police she was with Everett all evening and the whole night. But she wasn't. This woman who was working in the house says she was just closing the door to the servants' stairs, on her way up to her room, around ten o'clock, when she saw Grace leave her bedroom. She said Grace was real pale but not hysterical or crying or anything. She hurried down the stairs like she didn't want nobody to see her. Of course, didn't nobody official ever ask the woman what she'd seen, so she never told nobody official."

"That means Grace lied. He didn't really have an alibi."

"Oh, and that's not all. Your man Everett was seen by somebody other than you and Nate on the night the sheriff died. Miz Minnie's been talking your interest in these folks around. I got a call from Bennie Jackson, who drives a cab. He said he picked Everett up at the family's place in Farleigh and took him to the Bide-Away Motel out on Route Nine."

Blanche didn't need to ask the purpose of Everett's visit. The Bide-Away was a hangout for local prostitutes. Legitimate white motel-room seekers were sent to the Sleep-Well Motel, just down the road and owned by the same bunch of Farleigh businessmen. Of course, black inquirers and those with foreign accents were told both motels were full. Many of the Bide-Away's customers preferred to take a cab to and from the motel, particularly if their cars were distinctive ones. The motel parking lot fronted right on the highway.

"What time did Bennie drop him off?"

"After midnight. The paper said the sheriff died about three A.M. Plenty of time for Everett to get laid, leave, and go kill the sheriff," Ardell said. "I asked Bennie to check around and see if he could find out who took that sucker back home."

ELEVEN

B lanche was sweeping the front porch when Grace and Everett returned. Everett was the first one out of the car. The tightness around his eyes had increased. He strode quickly into the house. Grace walked slowly onto the porch. She had that tired-out and worn-to-a-frazzle look women often have after spending the morning with a peevish child. She seemed almost dazed.

"We'd like some lunch, after all, please, Blanche. Something quick, please."

Blanche followed Grace into the house. In the kitchen, she gathered the ingredients for a mushroom omelet and a green salad. It didn't look like they'd found Emmeline. That was undoubtedly enough to put their nerves on edge. But was there more? She put just a touch too much salt in the omelet and made the salad dressing a bit too tart. She knew a poorly seasoned meal could be just the irritant to snap a person's nerves and make them say or do something rash.

Despite the extra salt and vinegar, both Grace and Everett seemed to have swung from one extreme of appetite to the other. Neither of them had done more than sip coffee and crumble toast at breakfast. Now they ate as though they expected their meals to be cut off. They quickly finished the cold cucumber soup, and it was a good thing she'd made a six-egg omelet. They ate quickly and silently. But for all the attention they paid to the food, they might not have been eating at all. The air was full of argument. When Blanche had gone into the living room to tell them lunch was ready, Everett was speaking in a low, urgent tone, as though trying to convince Grace to do something she didn't want to do. Blanche had lingered outside the room before entering, hoping to hear what he was saying, but all she could catch was the hiss and pop of sparks flashing in the air, and Grace's attempts to dampen them. They'd stopped talking the moment Blanche entered. Everett was standing in the middle of the floor, his hands jammed deep in his pockets and his eyes sharp as butcher knives. Grace had pressed herself deep into her chair, as though pinned by a gale force wind.

Now Blanche moved dishes and cutlery without a clink and walked lightly around the room, drawing as little attention to herself as possible. She hoped the need to continue their fight would overwhelm their discretion.

"That will be all, Blanche. Thank you."

"Yes, sir." Blanche slipped through the swinging door to the kitchen. The rumble of his voice began before the door was fully closed. She decided not to listen from the pantry. There was a watchfulness in Everett that made her cautious. She wiped the counter and made herself a sandwich. Later, a soft click on the other side of the dining room door made her turn expectantly. Everett looked like a person with a bad case of heartburn.

"What did you want when you knocked on my aunt's door while we were out?"

"Excuse me, sir?" Blanche only half-pretended to be confused. She tried to think back to exactly what she'd done outside Emmeline's door. She couldn't take her eyes off him, even though he was the last person she wanted to see.

"Why did you knock on my aunt's door? What did you want?" His voice was as cold and hostile as his glare.

"I didn't. I didn't knock on the door. I mighta bumped it while I was vacuuming the hall, but I had no call to knock. No, sir." She held her voice firm and steady. She stood as still as she could, poised for his next question or move.

She could feel his eyes on her face. He reached up and ran his hands through his hair repeatedly, then let his arm drop.

"Perhaps she was dreaming," Everett said at last.

"Yes, sir."

Blanche smiled to herself and hummed her no-tune after he'd gone. It felt good to win a round with Everett and to be proven right about Emmeline's room being empty. But what a sneaky bastard! Still, he'd given her an opening. She was ready for Grace when she showed up later.

"Is your husband all right?" Blanche demanded to know before Grace was fully through the doorway.

Grace nearly dropped the heavy tray. "What do you mean? Why do you ask? What's happened?"

Blanche snatched the tray from Grace's hands and flounced to the sink in mock indignation. She banged the tray down hard enough for the dishes to clatter, then turned, hand on hip, toward Grace.

"He come in here accusing me of knocking on your aunt's door. As if I'd do such a thing after you told me not to bother her! I told him I didn't do it, but he acted like he didn't believe me. I don't appreciate being treated like I ain't telling the truth! I ain't got no reason to lie to him. He wasn't hisself, either. He acted... funny." She made the final word sound like incipient insanity. "Real funny," she added.

Grace drew herself up in a way that made Blanche think she was about to explode, but instead, tears welled in Grace's eyes. "I don't know what to do! I just don't!"

Blanche clenched her teeth and forced herself to approach Grace and gently pat her shoulder. "Now, ma'am, you just sit right down here." She eased Grace onto a chair, then left her side long enough to make her a glass of ice water in which she floated a slice of lemon.

"You keep on like this," she told Grace as she handed her the water, "and you're gonna make yourself sick." She fetched the tissues from the counter and handed them to Grace. "Anybody can see you're a kind, sensitive woman. But you got too much on your shoulders." Blanche's show of kindness brought on a fresh batch of tears. Blanche returned to her shoulder-patting position. "It's that aunt of yours, ain't it?" Blanche held her breath. She was hoping it would be easier to get Grace to talk about her aunt than about her husband.

Grace nodded her head in the affirmative. "She's gone."

Blanche fell back, with a look of what she hoped was surprise and distress on her face. "Gone? What…She passed?"

"No, oh, no! She's run off again!"

"What you mean 'again,' ma'am? Run off where?"

"It's not the first time. She…It's the drinking. She goes…She drinks with anyone who'll…" More sobs, until Grace heaved a great shuddering sigh and raised her head. "Please! Don't let him know I told you. He said it would be best not to…and to keep it from Mumsfield, too." Her eyes glittered behind her tears.

"That's all right, ma'am, I understand how it is, but it seems to me that he don't…" Blanche stopped and gave Grace a searching look, as if gauging whether it was safe to go on.

"What do you mean? What about my husband?"

"Well, ma'am, it just don't seem to me that he's all that much of a help to you, what with your aunt to look after and the house and all…"

Grace discreetly blew her nose and wiped her eyes. "Please, I don't want to…I can't discuss my husband…He…"

"Anything you say, ma'am. But it seems to me, what you need is a friend, somebody to help you with this mess."

As Blanche had hoped, her comment caused even more tears.

"Oh, God, I hope he hasn't done anything awful," Grace moaned. "I hope he hasn't…hurt anyone." She looked beseechingly up at Blanche.

"Hasn't what? Hurt who?" Blanche was in the back-patting business again.

"He's so…He gets so angry. After the sheriff left last time, Everett was in a rage. He said…he said he was going to put the sheriff out of his misery. And the next day…"

As much as she hated to do it, Blanche quickly raised her hand in a silencing gesture that startled Grace. A second later, the dining-room door swung open.

"What's taking you so long?"

Grace jumped at the sound of Everett's voice.

Blanche turned to face him, shielding Grace with her body, giving Grace a few seconds to pull her face together.

"We need to leave," he announced.

Grace rose slowly from her chair and followed her husband out of the room. She kept her head down to hide her tear-stained face. She gave Blanche a bleak look before the door swung shut behind her. It wasn't until they'd left the house that Blanche realized she hadn't told Grace about the call from Emmeline.

TWELVE

Mumsfield was hungry when he got back. He bubbled on about carburetors and other things that smelled of grease while Blanche sliced ham and tomatoes for sandwiches. "Your cousins have gone out again," Blanche told him.

"I know, Blanche. I heard them talking. They went to find that drunken old bitch." His voice was edged with something Blanche thought was anger. "Who is that drunken old bitch, Blanche?"

"Mumsfield, honey, do you know what it means to be an alcoholic?"

"Oh, yes, Blanche. Like Mr. Hoaglin, down at the garage. He always has a bottle that says 'Wild Turkey' in his back pocket. And sometimes he smells bad."

Blanche waited for him to give another, closer example, but he only looked at her expectantly.

"Don't you know someone else who drinks too much sometimes?"

Mumsfield was silent. Blanche could see him running through the list of his acquaintances searching for one with a drinking problem. "No, Blanche," he said at last.

Blanche sat down across the table from him. She extended her hands across the table toward him, palms up, although she didn't touch him. "Mumsfield, honey," she began, "sometimes, when people we love do something we don't like, we pretend the thing we didn't like didn't happen." She hesitated again, but he said nothing, only watched her face, waiting.

"Sometimes," Blanche went on, in a slightly different direction, "people who are close to us tell us not to believe things we know are happening. Do you understand, Mumsfield, honey?"

"Sure, Blanche," he told her without a moment's hesitation.

"Well, I think your Aunt Emmeline drinks too much gin sometimes and that's why she doesn't want to see you. And your Aunt Grace tells you your Aunt Emmeline is sick so you won't find out she's really drunk."

Mumsfield sprang forward in his chair. "No, Blanche! Aunt Emmeline does not drink too much!" He shook his head from side to side, not with vehemence but with certainty, like a person looking out on a sunny day while being told it's raining. "A little sherry for the blood, my boy, is all the strong drink one needs to imbibe," Mumsfield added in his Emmeline voice.

"Is that the way she sounds to you? She sounds different to me," Blanche challenged him.

"But she never talked to you, Blanche." Mumsfield gave her a sympathetic smile.

Blanche felt her face flush with embarrassment. Despite her contention that she had more respect for Mumsfield than his own people, she too had fallen into the trap of not really listening to what he was saying. He'd tried to tell her about Emmeline any number of times.

Blanche turned her head and stared out the window while she worked what Mumsfield had just told her into the mosaic of what she already knew. She chuckled to herself and at herself. So the fox was being outfoxed, she thought. All those tears! Could they really have been phony? Or had Grace decided she was in too far and wanted out? But why tell me the so-called Emmeline was out on a binge at all? Why trust an employee you didn't know very well with that information? Unless, of course, you wanted to keep her ignorant and on your side. At any rate, it was now obvious what the sheriff had had on Everett and why the sheriff had been killed. But how had the sheriff found out? She turned her head and looked at Mumsfield.

"Did you tell the sheriff that old drunk wasn't your Aunt Emmeline?"

"Yes, Blanche."

"What did he say?"

"He said Mumsfield shouldn't worry. He said Aunt Emmeline was safe and just fine, and that he would take care of everything and everything would be straightened out in a few days. He said Mumsfield should—"

"Should not tell Cousin Grace and Cousin Everett?"

"Secret, Blanche. Police business." The words burst from his mouth. She could see his shoulders rising in tension as her questions caused a frown to crease his forehead.

That rotten bastard! He must have really gotten his jollies putting this boy on. In this part of the country, people didn't bother to pretend the USA was a classless society. Now she understood why Mumsfield had taken the sheriff's death so hard. He'd had no one else to turn to once the sheriff was gone. He'd undoubtedly noticed that she didn't want to talk about his Aunt Emmeline. And even though the sheriff was dead, he couldn't go to Grace or Everett.

"Oh, baby, I'm so sorry."

"But where is Aunt Emmeline, Blanche? Mumsfield is...I am so worried about her." The tears he'd been trying to hold in came spilling down his cheeks.

"I don't know where she is, Mumsfield." It was only a partial lie. Now that she knew about the switch, she was almost sure Emmeline was dead, probably in the cellar in the house in town. Why else would they lock the door to the cellar when Mumsfield said the freezer and washing machine were kept down there? Blanche felt sick from having lived among these people.

"What exactly did you hear your cousins saying?" she asked him.

Mumsfield's face fell into the stony, speaking-in-tongues expression he always wore when he imitated people. The voice that now came out of his mouth was pure Grace, only this was the voice of a Grace whom Blanche had never seen, a Grace so angry her words sizzled.

"I told you she'd be more trouble than she's worth. But you insisted. Now she's out there staggering around the countryside about to..."

Mumsfield's voice slipped into a lower register and became Everett. "She won't get far."

"It doesn't matter how far she gets. What matters is who she meets, who she talks to," came the reply from Grace.

"Remember, Grace, she can't give us away without giving herself away as well. She won't talk."

"Perhaps not while she's sober. But how long do you think that will last?"

"It's too late to go over that. We'll look for her after breakfast," was Everett's reply.

Mumsfield paused and took a deep breath. When he spoke again it was in his own voice. "Is she dead, Blanche?"

Blanche watched him closely, not knowing quite what to expect. "I don't know for sure, Mumsfield, but we've got to find out."

"Yes, Blanche." He dried his eyes.

She took Archibald's phone numbers from her apron pocket. He was the one who'd accepted the phony Emmeline's signature. He had some stake in this, too. Her only other choice was to call the police. The idea of voluntarily putting herself in the hands of the sheriff's office didn't warrant a moment's thought. She went to the phone and dialed.

When the receptionist had finished turning the names of the partners in Archibald's law firm into a meaningless string of sounds, Blanche asked for Mr. Archibald Symington and was passed on to a more precise voice. This voice told her Archibald would be in conference for the rest of the day.

"Please tell him Miz Emmeline Carter would like to see him at her country place at his earliest possible convenience," Blanche told the woman on the phone. "And she asks that he please bring the letter she recently sent him."

The precise voice developed a coat of ice when Blanche asked her to repeat the message, but she'd been too well trained to take orders not to do it.

The woman who answered the phone at the second number, which Blanche assumed was Archibald's home number, was more interested in who Blanche was than in giving out information on when Archibald was expected to return. Blanche left the same message and hung up.

Now she could only wait. It was a hard prescription. Waiting for some prime-aged white man to show up and set things right had the ring of guaranteed failure. She sank slowly onto the chair across from Mumsfield.

Mumsfield moved his glass around on the table. He took a deep breath and let it out slowly.

"I'm scared, Blanche." He let go of his glass and stretched his damp, chilly fingers out toward her. Blanche gave his hands a squeeze.

"Me, too," she told him. "But we can't just sit here with our knees knocking. You gotta go get Archibald," she told him. "Those people in his office ain't paying me no mind."

Blanche fetched the phone book, looked up Archibald's office address, and wrote it down on half the sheet of paper she'd taken from Grace's room. "Here." She handed the paper to Mumsfield. "Anybody in town can tell you how to get there."

Mumsfield fidgeted in his chair. He shook his head from side to side.

"You want to know where your Aunt Emmeline is, don't you? You want to find out what happened to Nate, don't you?"

"Nate?" he asked.

"Somebody killed him." She watched his eyes widen.

"I can get a ride from the gas station," he told her. Blanche gave him a hug.

"But you mustn't talk to anyone else about it." He nodded his head in response. "And when you get there, make them take you right to Archibald, no matter where he is. Can you do that?"

Mumsfield began rocking from side to side. He swung his arms back and forth as he swayed. "I must see Cousin Archibald, now. Now! I must see Cousin Archibald, now. Now!" he chanted over and over, faster and faster. He looked as though he were on the verge of flying to pieces. Blanche wondered if she'd taxed him too much.

Just as abruptly as he'd begun, he stopped. "Like that?" he asked and gave her a mischievous grin. Blanche was truly impressed. She went with him to the front of the house and opened the door for him. She watched him walk down the drive and stared her growing affection for him in the face. She didn't like what she saw. But she knew it was useless to deny it. She believed that every person was unique. She also believed some people were more obviously special than others. And Mumsfield was very special, at least to her. She didn't know if he was able to connect with other people the way he did with her, but each time they talked, she came away feeling that if they just had the time, they could learn to talk without words.

For all his specialness and their seeming connectedness, Mumsfield was still a white man. She didn't want to shower concern on someone whose ancestors had most likely bought and sold her ancestors as though they were shoes or machines. Would she always find some reason—mental challenge, blindness, sheer incompetence—to nurture people who had been raised to believe she had no other purpose in life than to be their "girl"? Had the slavers stamped mammyism into her genes when they raped her great-grandmothers? If they had, she was determined to prove the power of will over blood. When Mumsfield was out of sight, she slowly closed the door and thought about her next move. Given what a sly boots Grace had turned out to be, Blanche decided to give her room a more thorough search.

She began with Grace's closet—a study in organization—and slipped her hand beneath and among drawers full of panties and bras, all in the same heavy cream-colored silk. She patted nightgowns and probed stacks of slips until she had only one more drawer to search.

When she opened the last drawer, a hint of Grace's floral perfume scented the air. Neatly folded scarves rested upon one another like banked, multicolored clouds. Blanche gently lifted a few of them and held them lightly in her left hand. She wormed her right hand through the scarves to the bottom and back of the drawer. She found only more scarves. One of them managed to become snagged on the cuff of her rubber glove.

It was a large silk square, with a cream background and big pink and mauve flowers with dusky-green leaves, like overblown gardenias. It was at the same time exotic and Victorian. Blanche complimented Grace on her choice. She folded the scarf so that a subtle pink blossom was centered on top. The color caught Blanche's attention and held her eyes. It reminded her of something she'd been trying to remember. Something about the night Nate was murdered. Something…

Everett sneaking the limo down the drive. She saw him clearly as the car moved slowly away from the house. His arm on the window ledge was blue-white in the moonlight. Blue-white. She stared down at the scarf in her hands. Her body understood what this meant long before her brain patched the truth together. She remembered the creases in the sleeves of the pink jacket, turned back to accommodate shorter arms. She shivered. The front door slammed with a bang. Blanche dropped the scarf and headed for the back stairs.

Grace was in the kitchen, leaning weakly against the wall. For the first time, Blanche noticed that Grace's eyes didn't match. One eye—the right—was almost almond-shaped, but her left eye was round and unwavering as a blue marble. Grace began to whimper. But there were no tears in her left eye. Her hair was full of twigs and bits of leaves. There were scratches, like strips of raw meat, on her face and neck. She was holding her right elbow in her left hand, as though she was hurt. Dirt and twigs stuck to her skirt and blouse. "What happened?" Blanche asked her.

Grace's face twisted as though the question caused her pain. She pushed herself away from the wall. She limped to the table, leaned heavily on it, then sank slowly into a chair. "What happened?" Blanche asked her once again.

Grace shook back her hair in one of those white-girl gestures that used to wrench Blanche's heart, when she was young and sure that being nappy-headed was a hindrance to being beautiful. Now she recognized the gesture as a play for time.

"He...he said he was going to kill us both. He was crazy, babbling....He said it was the only way. I grabbed the wheel.... Oh, God!" She looked up wildly at Blanche. There were tears in both eyes now. Blanche took a step back from the table. "It was so awful. I was so frightened. I can't tell you how frightened I was!"

Blanche felt like someone who'd been tricked by a red spade. She'd been too busy looking down on Grace to notice those eyes. And how had she allowed herself to believe that a person bent on unseen murder in the dark would wear a pink jacket—unless it was meant to be seen by a witness? But then, why kill the witness? As a person whose living depended on her ability to read character, Blanche was both shocked and frightened. She couldn't survive with muddled wits.

"I've injured my arm." Grace held her arm out for Blanche's inspection. Blanche knew she was expected to go to Grace, to make soothing sounds and call on the Lord for protection and mercy while she fluttered about, gathering first-aid items and insisting she be allowed to call the doctor and the police. It was the combination of her memory of Everett's pale arm resting on the car window ledge and Grace's unwavering left eye that made her step back instead.

"You killed Nate." The accusation jumped unbidden from Blanche's mouth with calm certainty.

"Please," Grace moaned. "My arm." Once again she held her arm out to Blanche. Blanche neither moved nor spoke. She stared directly into Grace's eyes. After a few moments, Grace chuckled and relaxed against the back of the chair. She let her arm fall gracefully to the table. A tight-lipped, bittersweet smile played across her mouth. She looked like somebody who'd just lost a poker game she'd thought was all tied up.

"You did kill him, didn't you? You might as well tell me. You're planning to kill me anyway. Me and the boy. You going to burn this house down, too?" Both anger and fear were present in her voice.

"You surprise me."

Blanche knew exactly what Grace meant. As far as the Graces of the world were concerned, hired hands didn't think, weren't curious, or observant, or capable of drawing even the most obvious conclusions. When would they learn? "Why did you kill him?"

"Nate." Grace shrugged as if she couldn't think of a subject more boring.

Blanche clenched her teeth against the urge to call her a murderous bitch. It was information, not a fight, that she was after. Was it true that murderers liked to brag about what they'd done? "Well, you sure had me fooled," she told Grace.

Grace smiled, but she didn't start talking. Blanche primed the pump. "Of course, Nate wasn't the only one. Where's the real Emmeline?"

Grace rose from the table. "*Miss* Emmeline," she corrected. She moved around the room touching everything she passed: chair, canister, table, curtain, door, stove, counter, as though she were taking inventory.

"She needn't have been so difficult." Grace might have been talking about a child who'd refused to finish lunch. She circled the table and approached Blanche. As she inched along, she continued to touch items in the room—the same items, Blanche thought, that she'd fingered before. Blanche moved with her so that the distance between them never narrowed. Grace stopped when she came parallel to the sink. "She should have listened, tried to understand how important it was to me to..." Grace's words trailed off as she stared at the sink.

"To have Mumsfield's money?" Blanche took no care to keep her feelings out of her voice.

Grace turned scornful eyes on her. "It's not *his* money. It's my family's money! My great-granddaddy..." She turned toward the sink. "I was her closest relative. Her closest *normal* relative, at any rate. Just how did she think it would look?" There was fire in her voice. She turned the handles of the hot and cold water taps, tested the water temperature, and fiddled with the knobs until she was satisfied. She picked up the bottle of dishwashing liquid and stared at the print on the back of it. She poured about a teaspoon-fill of the pearly white liquid into her left palm, added some water, and seemed totally absorbed in watching the suds grow thick and creamy between her hands.

"You killed your aunt when you and Mumsfield went into town to church. That's why you wouldn't let him go into the house, isn't it?"

"I told him she had a heart attack while I was with her in the cellar. The jackass believed me!" Grace washed the dabs of mud and bits of grass from her arms and hands.

"You mean your husband?"

"I really made you believe I loved him, didn't I?" She threw back her head and opened her mouth wide to let out a brash, blaring laugh that startled Blanche. "Oh, he's been useful. Like a veil, a bit of camouflage. But love that fool?" She belted out another brassy laugh.

"Why'd you marry him if you think he's such a fool?"

"I told you. He was useful." Grace reached over and ripped a handful of paper towels from the roll hanging on the wall. "It was cruel of Daddy to leave me money only if I married. He wanted me to have a keeper, someone to…watch me." She thoroughly dried her hands, then used the towels to brush the dust and twigs from her clothes and shoes.

"But I found someone who wouldn't…There are more ways to tie a man to you than sex and children." She examined her hands closely, turning them this way and that, checking the nails, pushing at a cuticle.

"Like helping him kill his wife?" Blanche took another couple of steps away from Grace.

"You *have* been busy." Grace took a couple of steps toward Blanche.

"Is that how you tied him to you? By helping him get rid of his wife?" Blanche took a step backward.

Grace guffawed. "Help him? That's hardly what happened. You've got it wrong." Grace's voice had the same peeved yet triumphant tone she'd used when she'd first ushered Blanche past the gate into the house in town. "I always hated her, with her whiny voice and all that pretty hair. Always dimpling up to Daddy, stealing my…"

Blanche remembered what Nate had said about nasty rumors when Grace's young cousin drowned in the pond. She realized that she and Grace were talking about two different victims. Careful, she warned herself. "Your daddy liked your cousin better than you, didn't he?"

Bright red spots appeared high on Grace's cheeks. "No! No! I was Daddy's favorite, always. He…" She stopped in mid-sentence with the look on her face of someone who'd just waked to find herself in an unfamiliar room.

Her stillness was chilling. Blanche swallowed hard. "What about your husband? Were you his favorite, too? Or did you have to help him kill his first wife in order to get him?"

Grace looked startled but didn't speak. She seemed to be listening to or for something. The silence in the room was like gas building toward an explosion.

"I thought you didn't love him." Blanche's voice was high and loud to her own ears. "Why did you kill his wife? You could have bought yourself some other man."

"Because I hated her! Hated her!" Grace bent her knees and pounded on her thighs with tightly clenched fists. She shouted each word slowly and distinctly. "She was just like…"

"Your cousin grown up." Blanche completed Grace's sentence, then recoiled from the woman just as she did from slugs and other slimy creatures. She held her face perfectly still, determined to show nothing of what she felt to this woman who had been mad and murderous even as a child. Keep the bitch talking and bragging, she cautioned herself, and hope Mumsfield and Archibald get their asses here in a hurry! She willed herself to relax. She could play this conversation, push enough of Grace's buttons to keep her fixated on herself, as opposed to what Blanche was sure she'd come for. "If you don't love him, why are you trying to protect him?" she challenged Grace.

"He wasn't even there!" Grace bellowed at the top of her voice. Flecks of foamy spittle collected in the corners of her mouth. Blanche took two more steps away from her.

"He didn't even know I'd killed her until after we were married."

"So the alibi was really for yourself!"

Grace poked her chest out a little further. "A master stroke, if I say so myself. He was under suspicion for murdering Jeannette. I knew he would be. I supplied him with a badly needed alibi, thereby proving my undying devotion to him and providing an alibi for myself as well. Of course, he was happy to marry me when he found out about the money. It's the only way Everett can support himself. He didn't get a dime of Jeannette's money. Her family saw to that. I knew they would. By marrying me, he got access to a fresh supply of money. Not just mine, but Aunt Emmeline's as well. Everett needs a lot of money to be happy. We both do. I told him there was enough for both of us." She rolled her eyes and gave Blanche a conspiratorial look. "And they say it's sex that clouds men's minds!" Grace shook her head and smiled as though Everett and all his money-hungry brothers were just a bunch of devilish little tykes. She ran her hands through her hair in a way that was reminiscent of Everett.

"Where is he?" Blanche asked again.

Grace didn't answer immediately. When she did speak, it was not to answer Blanche's question. "A very useful, if greedy, man was Everett...but not a very intelligent man," she added with a low chuckle. She tucked her blouse more firmly into her waistband and straightened her skirt. "Am I being redundant?" She gave Blanche a cold, speculative look. "Do you know what a redundancy is? I wonder." Grace grinned a smug, derisive grin.

Blanche associated Grace's mocking smile with every white person who'd ever ridiculed her for what she was and was not. For a moment, her mouth went sour with the taste of ignorance. She'd look up "redundancy" the first chance she got. If she got a chance. In the meantime, she had no intention of letting Grace know that she had struck a nerve.

"Where is he?" she pressed.

"I'll get to that in due time," Grace told her. "I'm enjoying this. After all, anything I tell you is bound to remain a secret, isn't it?"

The smile that accompanied this question was as cold as the dead of winter. Its meaning was quite plain and no surprise. I wonder what she thinks I'm going to be doing while she's trying to kill me? Blanche gave Grace a searching look. Grace had no obvious weapon and no place to hide one that Blanche could see. It was possible Grace didn't know which kitchen drawers held knives or other sharp instruments. But I know, Blanche thought. She wore the knowledge that she was a quick movement away from a meat cleaver like armor against Grace.

"Yes, a redundancy." Grace picked up the thread of her monologue and told Blanche how she and Everett had drugged

Emmeline and left her tied to a cot in the basement. "She was quite comfortable," Grace added, as if to demonstrate her familial concern. "It was his idea. It began when he found that woman."

"You mean the look-alike?"

Grace affirmed Blanche's question with a flicker of her eyelids.

"Who is she, anyway?"

"That's none of your affair." Grace gave her one of those employer-has-spoken looks to which demure silence was the only correct response.

"All this shit is my affair. You made sure of that when you killed Nate."

Instead of answering Blanche's question, Grace outlined the plan Everett had put to her—drugging Emmeline and replacing her with the look-alike for the signing of the new will, then returning Emmeline to her bed later the same night. "I knew it wouldn't work, of course. I can't imagine how that fool convinced himself that sharp old bitch could actually be convinced she'd slept for a whole day or had forgotten it! But, of course, I had my own plan, and it worked beautifully!" Grace glowed with pride. "I dissolved the pills in her soup and Everett carried her to the basement. Then we closed the house and came down here with that woman." Grace spoke in a one, two, three, that's-how-you-make-a-good-apple-pie voice that made Blanche queasy.

Grace was on the move again, pacing the kitchen in even, unhurried steps. Blanche matched her step for step. Grace picked up the salt shaker from the counter. "I found the hypodermic needle in Aunt's room months ago." She put the salt shaker back on the counter so that it was precisely aligned with the pepper mill. "Dr. Pritchard left it behind. He never came looking for it." Her voice registered her indignation at the doctor's carelessness.

"What was in the hypodermic?"

"Nothing!" Grace straightened a pot holder on its hook until it hung at the same angle as the pot holder on the corresponding hook. "Just air." She stared at Blanche as though daring her to comment.

"But didn't your husband suspect something? I mean, first his wife and then your aunt?"

There needed to be a word other than "smile" to describe the toothy leer on Grace's face. "He was too greedy to suspect anything, too self-serving. He had no more use for her. She'd cut his allowance." The giggle that curled around Grace's words was almost girlish. "Anyway, I told him I'd loved him since childhood. The same drivel I told you. He believed everything I told him until…"

Blanche was aware of Grace's continued use of the past tense when she talked about Everett. She was also aware of how easily, and for what flimsy motives, Grace was prepared to kill. "Until what?" she wanted to know. "Where is he?"

Grace shrugged and tossed her head.

"Was the sheriff's death what made Everett stop believing you?"

"You know about the sheriff!" Grace's voice held the kind of surprise a parent shows when a young child does something precocious. "But you'll never guess how!" she laughed and actually paused, to give Blanche an opportunity to try to guess, which Blanche declined.

"With the one weapon I knew would work." She ran her hands slowly down her sides and moved her hips with a sensuousness that surprised Blanche. She didn't think Grace had that much juice in her. Grace's retelling of how she'd convinced the sheriff to drive to Oman's Bluff was much like many other stories Blanche had heard from other women about how they'd made some man pay for walking around with his brain in his penis. Blanche had a few such stories of her own. Her familiarity with the weapon made the murderous account of this privileged, protected, so-called upper-class, and at least superficially uptight woman wielding the world's oldest weapon even more frightening, more chilling.

"It was as though he'd forgotten everything he knew about me," Grace told her.

Yes, Blanche thought, that's always a part of it.

"I didn't let him know I was in the back seat until we were on the highway. He nearly jumped through the windshield when I popped up behind him. Oh, but that was nothing compared to his reaction when I laid my brassiere on his shoulder! He ran right off the road!" Grace's words were made almost unintelligible by her laughter. "I want to settle our problem in a way I hope you can't refuse, Sheriff," Grace whispered in a soft voice full of the genteel Georgia accent that was normally only a ghost of a presence in her speech.

Blanche imagined the sheriff congratulating himself on his good fortune as his brain swelled to full attention in his clammy shorts.

"I wouldn't let him stop the car until we got to Oman's Bluff. And, of course, I kept out of his reach. I had no intention of letting him put his disgusting hands on me!" Grace shivered delicately at the very idea. "I told him I wanted things to be just right. I leaned over and whispered all the things we'd do to each other once we got to Oman's Bluff. You should have seen him! He kept turning his head to look at me, as if he wanted to make sure I wouldn't disappear. His eyes reminded me of a child seeing its first Christmas tree. He kept licking his lips until they were all shiny." Grace shuddered and paused.

Blanche braced herself for this account of exactly what Grace had done next, while in another part of her mind, she had yet to believe she was actually standing here listening to the details of murders told to her by the person who'd committed them.

"It was really quite simple." Grace might have been describing how she'd contrived a particularly elegant flower arrangement. "When he began to climb into the back seat, I picked up the wrench from the seat beside me and..." She made a sideways swiping motion once, then twice more. Each stroke was accompanied by a deep, satisfied grunt. Blanche winced. She saw the sheriff slump, half his body hanging over the top of the front seat, like a doll tossed carelessly by a child. Grace's eyes gleamed.

"It's all gravel up there, you know, so I didn't have to worry about footprints. I simply drove the car to the edge, got out, and…" Grace made a long pushing gesture. Sinews stood out in her neck and arms as she pushed at the big car. But there was a great deal of strength in those arms, enough to cause the wheels of the car to turn slowly, the car to inch forward. Grace completed her pushing gesture with a breathy "Unhh." Her lips were parted and seemed fuller; color enlivened her face.

"I don't believe you!" Blanche nearly shouted at Grace. "I think you're trying to protect Everett!"

"Him! That slug? Where would he get the courage?" Grace's voice was rising. "But he makes a perfect suspect, don't you think?" Her sly grin was back.

"So you put the sheriff's handcuffs in Everett's blanket chest."

"You *are* a nosy one, aren't you? Not that it's going to do you any good."

"I still don't believe you. Everett killed Nate and the sheriff."

Blanche stirred Grace's irritation at having her exploits chalked up to Everett. She was even beyond responding to Blanche's use of his first name.

"Your friend Nate kept a very tidy place. Quite quaint, actually."

Blanche's hands became fists. Her face and neck were suddenly hot. "Why did you kill him? He thought it was your husband he'd seen on the path to Oman's Bluff, not you. Isn't that what you planned?"

"Oman's Bluff?" Grace repeated, as though she'd never heard of the place. "It had nothing to do with Oman's Bluff. That jacket provides all the evidence the police will need that my husband killed the sheriff.

"It was that woman! How was I to know Nate would recognize her? They say you people always know one of your own, no matter how light-skinned. But she was so white...Of course, I should have thought...He'd been here so long."

The idea that all black people recognized each other, no matter how diluted their African blood, appealed to Blanche, but she was proof it wasn't so. It certainly hadn't occurred to her that there was any ancestral connection between her and that old drunk.

"But how did you know he recognized her?"

Grace gave her a you're-not-going-to-believe-this look. "Missy, I know it ain't none a my business, and 'scuse me for sayin' it, but that man of yourn is gonna git you in a heap a trouble," she said in a broad and ridiculing imitation of Nate.

The thought of Nate losing his life because he had tried to help Grace made Blanche tingle and smart as though all of her limbs had been asleep. "What did you do to him?" Her lips stung with rage.

"I dropped my handbag," Grace told her. "Of course, he rushed to pick it up. He never saw the wrench in my other hand, in the fold of my skirt. The same wrench...When he bent down..." Grace giggled.

Blanche flinched from the possibility that Nate had lived long enough to know that he was about to die for trying to help someone who'd never seen him as anything but a dog's midwife. The thought of Nate's last moments sent Blanche moving toward Grace with a swift determination that momentarily paralyzed Grace. Her eyes widened, but she couldn't seem to move. When she finally gathered the presence of mind to take a step away from Blanche, it was too late.

The pain that shot up Blanche's arm as her knuckles made contact with Grace's lips and teeth was so satisfying it made her "Aah" with pleasure. But she had only a moment in which to savor it.

Although Blanche had struck her hard enough to rattle her teeth, Grace didn't stagger. No moan or scream passed her lips.

She didn't bother to wipe the blood dripping down her cream-colored silk blouse.

Oh, shit! Blanche suddenly remembered old Miz Carter, who finally went all the way round the bend and took off all of her clothes in the main rotunda of the statehouse. Six attendants and a straitjacket were needed to get her in the ambulance, even though she was ninety years old and thin as a pencil. And Grace had more than the superhuman strength of the mad on her side.

She had the drawer open and the carving knife in hand before Blanche could fully register what was happening. In Grace's hand, that familiar cooking tool became something out of a barroom brawl—slim, curved, and mean-looking. The sight of it momentarily dissolved all of her courage. Blanche was running for the door by the time Grace raised the knife and roared like a wild and angry beast. Blanche flung a kitchen chair behind her as she raced for the swinging door. In the dining room she hurled another chair, blocking the door on both sides. Grace cursed as she stumbled over the first chair.

Blanche threw open the front door, then ran up the stairs. Grace bellowed as she ran to the front door. She held the knife in both hands, her arms extended as though the knife were a divining rod that would lead her to Blanche.

Blanche looked down the upstairs hall. The house slammed all its doors in her face. You can't hide in here, it told her. Grace had known the house since she was a child. All its secret spaces were open to her. And when she finds me, Blanche thought, and honored the urge to check her back.

Grace was walking slowly up the stairs. She smiled up at Blanche as though they were long-lost friends. She held the knife as though she knew just how to thrust and rip with it. Blanche was rooted to the spot, mesmerized by Grace's wide, wild eyes. Grace was nearly at the top of the stairs before Blanche turned and ran down the back stairs, out the back door, and into the woods.

The woods around the house were thick with underbrush. There were places where only a small animal could penetrate. Spiky green fingers ripped at Blanche's ankles and calves. She had no idea how far the woods went on, so she didn't want to lose sight of the house. She looked for a tree to climb but couldn't find one with low limbs. From the corner of her eye she saw Grace running out the back door.

Blanche fell to her knees behind a bush and tried to slow her breathing. Through a chink in the shrubbery she watched Grace jerk her head and upper body from side to side, slashing about with the knife and looking crazily around the yard. Her arms swung way out from her body as she snapped first one way and then the other like a mechanical toy gone haywire. Then she abruptly stopped her frantic movements and headed for the shed at the foot of the yard.

"Are you in there, bitch?" she shouted in a voice that could have belonged to a man, a big, mean man. Grace kicked the shed door open and flung herself inside. Blanche could hear her throwing things about, cursing and screaming, and laughing in a high, eerie way.

Blanche felt something akin to shame. First some pervert ran her out of New York, then the law ran her into this mess, and now she was running away from a crazy-assed white woman! It didn't feel right. It didn't feel right at all.

Grace came out of the shed and looked quickly from side to side. Blanche fought the instinct to run. She took a deep breath, relaxed, took another breath, and felt her heart begin to beat a little more slowly. She could see that Grace's face was deep pink, and only tearing at her hair could have made it stand out in those spiky clumps. The fear that had pounded through Blanche's body while she was running like a panicked beast, now quieted. She imagined she heard Grace's ragged breathing above the chirping and squawking of birds.

Grace stomped through Nate's cabbages to the edge of the woods on the other side of the yard, diagonally across from where Blanche was hiding. She began inching slowly sideways, parallel to the woods. She was moving in Blanche's direction. The knife blade shone white in the sunlight. Blanche couldn't see Grace's face, but she didn't need to. Grace's whole body, the slowness of her motions and the utter stillness of her pauses, spoke of looking for the movement that didn't fit, listening for the sound that didn't belong.

Running from her was not the answer. Blanche shifted her position until her damp knees were off the ground. She assumed a deep and surprisingly comfortable squat, legs spread and her butt balanced in between. She felt somehow strengthened. She breathed in deep drafts of the dirt-and-green-smelling woods and looked around for a stone. She found a large pine cone. She hefted it to make sure it was weighty enough. She rose slowly and aimed the pine cone to the right of Grace's back.

Grace spun in the direction of the cone cracking to the ground. She crouched low and weaved her upper body from side to side, like a snake scoping prey. "I see you! You can't hide from me!" She crashed into the woods in the area where the cone had fallen.

Blanche changed her hiding place. She was now standing somewhat deeper in the woods, surrounded by bushes and saplings. Grace continued to worry the spot where she'd heard the sound. Blanche began moving toward the shed. She moved as quietly as possible, although it wasn't necessary. She could hear Grace thrashing about. Every once in a while Grace bellowed Blanche's name, along with some other names—like "whore," "nigger bitch," and "black slut," names Blanche had long ago learned had nothing to do with her and everything to do with the person from whose mouth they came. "She don't even pronounce them right," Blanche whispered to herself.

Blanche slipped into the shed. Grace had made quite a mess. Shards of broken clay pots mingled with the spilled guts of a bag of peat moss in the middle of the floor. Blanche stepped over a long board, plant stakes, and assorted debris. She turned and picked up the board. It was about three feet long and three inches wide. She held it like a squared-off baseball bat. She went to the shed door and used the stick to push it as hard as she could, so that the door swung out and slammed against the side of the shed with a crash like a gunshot blast. She stepped to the side of the doorway and waited.

It didn't take long. Grace was there in seconds, snorting and grunting like a wild pig. Half-formed curses and nearly incoherent insults foamed out of her mouth. Blanche took a deep breath, widened her stance, and hefted the board in both hands. As Grace's right foot and head appeared through the doorway, Blanche pivoted her body and pictured Grace's head as a large baseball.

The blow sent Grace sprawling backward to lie spread-eagled on the ground in front of the shed. Her right shoe lay on its side just inside the door. The knife skittered off into the cabbages. Blanche stood in the doorway staring out and down at Grace. A slow, satisfied grin spread over Blanche's face. She'd never been sure that talking back to her employers, and using their front rooms and first names, was enough to protect her against Darkies' Disease. It could be picked up like a virus, and her concern for Mumsfield had seemed like a symptom. But Grace's body lying unconscious on the ground was proof enough of her own mental health.

She stepped over Grace's legs and gingerly felt for a pulse in the woman's throat. Grace's skin was cool and clammy. Her pulse was strong. Blanche sank down on the shed step, next to Grace's feet, and balanced the board across her knees. She watched as the bruises below Grace's eyes became two glorious shiners and the tissues around her nose began to swell. Broken, Blanche diagnosed. Something to remember Nate by, she told Grace's unconscious body.

THIRTEEN

Blanche was still sitting on the shed stoop with a faint grin on her face when Archibald's car zoomed up the drive and screeched to a halt.

"Out here!" she shouted when she heard feet running toward the house.

Archibald hurried down the yard and knelt beside Grace. He picked up her wrist and lifted her eyelid as though he'd been trained as a doctor instead of a lawyer. Mumsfield came and stood close to Blanche and took her hand. His eyes seemed to be asking her something, but Blanche's mind wasn't moving fast enough to catch the question.

"What's happened here?" Archibald demanded once he'd felt Grace's pulse.

"Did you bring that letter? Did you read it?" Blanche asked him.

"What's happened here, I said!"

"She fell," Blanche told him. Until he read that letter, she wasn't going to say anything.

Archibald looked from Blanche to the board across her knees but didn't comment. He don't want to know any more than I want to tell him, Blanche realized.

"Where is Cousin Emmeline?" Archibald's tone was an accusation.

"Do you really want to talk about that now?" Blanche asked him.

Archibald looked from Blanche to Mumsfield, who was staring down at Grace with a look of shock and confusion on his face. "Perhaps you're right." He turned his full attention to reviving Grace, who was beginning to stir.

Mumsfield moved closer to Blanche's side. She could feel the heat from his body. "You need to read that letter," she told Archibald.

Grace groaned. Archibald leaned down to help her to her feet. They were like two drunken dancers. Each time he tried to help her up, Grace's weight pulled him off-balance.

"Give me a hand!" Archibald called out. Blanche snorted. Mumsfield held Blanche's hand a little tighter. Neither of them moved.

Archibald circled behind Grace, put his arms under her armpits, and heaved. Weaving and slipping sideways, Archibald finally hoisted Grace onto her feet. She was rocky, but she was upright. Her eyes were mere slits in puffy purple flesh. She looked around with a puzzled air, as though trying to figure out where she was and how she had gotten there. Her knees continued to buckle. She clutched Archibald for support. Blanche was delighted. If the sounds Grace was making were any indication, she was feeling as bad as she looked. Blanche felt new energy flow through her limbs at the sight of her handiwork.

Grace steadied herself with Archibald's help and peered at Blanche. "She...she..." Grace looked beseechingly up at Archibald and pointed at Blanche. Grace's face was stormy and indignant. "She...she..." Grace tried again, seeming more and more agitated. Then, without warning, her eyes glazed over as though she'd packed herself up and gone away, leaving her body behind. She shuffled docilely toward the back door, leaning heavily on Archibald's arm.

Blanche told Mumsfield to wait in the kitchen. She followed Archibald and Grace into the living room. Archibald settled Grace on the sofa and went to the hall phone. Blanche kept a skeptical eye on Grace. She seemed passive enough, but there was a glint in the back of her eyes when she looked at Blanche that made Blanche wonder how much of her zombie act was just that. Blanche could hear the urgency in Archibald's voice as he gave orders for a doctor and an ambulance. When he hung up the receiver, Blanche went to speak to him. "Have you read the letter yet?"

"I don't know what you're talking about. What's been going on here?"

It was exactly the situation she'd most feared. There was no letter. The look-alike had run off. Everett was dead in a ravine somewhere and Grace was too crackers, or wily, to talk or be held responsible for what she'd done. And guess who was left holding the bag?

"I'd better call the sheriff," Archibald announced.

"Grace killed Nate and the sheriff."

"Now, you look here, you…"

Blanche cut him off. "You let an imposter sign Emmeline's will, and you'd better check the cellar in the house in town before you call anybody."

Archibald stared at Blanche but he didn't interrupt her while she told him all that she knew and guessed. The doctor Archibald had called arrived in an unmarked van with two orderlies. Mumsfield came to the living room when he heard the doorbell. He seemed both repelled and fascinated by the doctor's probing and pressing of Grace's nose and face and her whimpers of pain. He took a few steps into the living room, fear and confusion etching age into his face. Blanche led him back to the kitchen.

Archibald went to the kitchen, once Grace had been taken away—to someplace private, Blanche was sure. His skin was gray and dry, as though someone had recently relieved him of a large quantity of blood.

"Please stay with the boy until I return," he said to Blanche. He turned and left the room before either she or Mumsfield could speak. Blanche motioned for Mumsfield to stay put and be quiet. She waited until Archibald had had enough time to clear the pantry and the dining room, then followed him.

Archibald went straight to the phone in the hall and made a call that Blanche did her damnedest to overhear. She heard enough to know that it was the wife of the attorney general to whom he spoke and addressed as "Cousin Julia." Blanche supposed this was less illegal than speaking to the attorney general, should "the whole unfortunate matter," as Archibald described it, ever come to light. Which he, of course, was committed to avoiding at all costs. He then described how the family could and should cover up any and all crimes. And they say there are some things money can't buy! Blanche thought Archibald left the house by the front door. Blanche went back to the kitchen.

She sank heavily onto a kitchen chair, propped her elbows on the table, and buried her face in her hands. She needed to think. She felt as though pieces of her were scattered around the place. She wished Mumsfield would go away, but she sensed that he needed her company. She closed her eyes and heard rather than saw Mumsfield fetching glasses and the pitcher of lemonade. He sat in the chair directly across from her. They were both quiet for a moment.

"Is Aunt Emmeline dead, Blanche?" Mumsfield's voice was low and exceedingly calm. Blanche wondered what it was costing him to keep it that way. She'd hoped to avoid this. She'd hoped Archibald would be the one to break the news.

"Is she, Blanche? Please tell me. I trust you, Blanche."

"Yes, baby. She's dead." Blanche looked into his face and saw new lines. It was no longer a boy's face. He lowered his head as he began to sob. When he was calm enough, he wiped his face and surprised her by asking for details of his aunt's death.

Blanche gave him a simplified version of what Grace had told her—how she and Everett had set out to get control of Emmeline's money by having someone sign her name to a new will, a will everyone approved of and, therefore, no one would question, a will that made Grace and Everett Mumsfield's financial guardians and put Emmeline's money under their control. She didn't add what she suspected Grace had planned for him.

"I don't know who that other woman was, exactly, but I'm sure she's kin to you," she responded to Mumsfield's question. She couldn't bring herself to mention Emmeline's being tied to a cot, or the air bubble Grace had injected into his probably struggling aunt. "Your cousins locked your Aunt Emmeline in the basement and she died there," she told him. This was the second time in less than an hour that she'd gone out of her way to protect him.

FOURTEEN

Archibald came directly to the kitchen when he returned. He found Blanche and Mumsfield still sitting at the table sipping lemonade. A slight tremor shook Archibald's hand as he reached for a kitchen chair. He leaned heavily, wearily, on the back of the chair before slowly seating himself. He tried to form a smile for Mumsfield, but his lips failed in their attempt to turn upward and his eyes were too bewildered to participate. After a few moments, he asked Mumsfield to please leave the room so that he could talk privately with Blanche. Blanche noted Mumsfield's struggle to defy Archibald. In the end, he lost. "You won't leave, will you, Blanche?" he asked before stepping out the back door.

"No one's leaving this house. You can be sure of that," Archibald cut in before Blanche could speak. He took an immaculate handkerchief from his breast pocket and dabbed at his brow. "I simply can't believe it. Poor Cousin Emmeline. To die like that!"

But his grief wasn't such that he couldn't attend to the necessary details. He made Blanche repeat everything she'd already told him about what Everett and Grace had done—with his unwitting help. He had the good grace to blush during the telling of that part of the story.

"Who is she, anyway?" Blanche asked him, referring to Emmeline's imposter.

Archibald bristled. "I don't believe…That is to say, I'm not at liberty to discuss family…"

"Look," Blanche interrupted, "I could have been killed by a member of this family. I got a right to know!"

Archibald relented. "I'd never seen her before that night I mistook her for Cousin Emmeline. Of course, I didn't realize... I'd heard of her...Family gossip...really remarkable resemblance. She would have fooled anyone who knew Emmeline. Anyone. And she seemed ill. I'm very susceptible to germs, and my eyes... I'm not attempting to exonerate myself, but..." He took his glasses from his breast pocket, polished them, and set them gently on his nose. "I should wear them all the time." He blinked at Blanche, who said nothing. She folded her arms and prepared to repeat her question, but he went on without prodding.

"She's the daughter of Great-uncle Robert, Cousin Emmeline's father. Her mother was their house maid. They say that as a child she looked so much like Aunt Emmeline—who looked exactly like her daddy—that Aunt Clarissa, who was Aunt Emmeline's mother, made Great-uncle Robert get mother and child out of the county. She married a local sharecropper. I don't recall hearing what happened to her after that. I think the child's name was Lucille or Lucinda, or something of that sort." Archibald's lips formed a straight, taut line, like a pale, thin, tightly interlocked zipper he had no intention of opening again on this matter.

"Look," Blanche told him, "I want to know what all this business is about. I could have gone to the police. By now it might be spread all over the newspapers."

Blanche hadn't expected Archibald to take kindly to her tone or the content of her message. His sharp intake of breath and the rising color in his cheeks confirmed her perception. She turned from Archibald toward the kitchen door.

"Where is Aunt Emmeline?" Mumsfield closed the door firmly behind him and looked from Blanche to Archibald and back at Blanche.

Blanche had been so concentrated on Archibald and what she wanted and needed to know from him that she'd literally forgotten Mumsfield was outside. She wondered if he'd been listening at the window. Archibald cleared his throat in what Blanche suspected was a play for time. "Brace yourself, my boy," he began.

"I know she's dead. I know that," Mumsfield interrupted. There was an impatience in his voice Blanche had never heard before. "Did you take her out of the cellar?" He didn't bother to wipe at his tears. "She shouldn't be down there. She…"

"Her body has been seen to. Been taken to…" Archibald sank deeper into his chair. "It's so hard to take in, to understand…" He shook his head like a man who'd just been punched.

Blanche understood Archibald's shock, but she was much more interested in Mumsfield. She hated the way misery and pain seemed to make people stronger in ways that good fortune rarely appeared to do, but she was glad for Mumsfield's sake. No matter how all of this turned out, she was sure he'd survive. Mumsfield caught her eye and gave her a grave half-smile.

"Now tell us the rest," she said, turning to Archibald. "Tell us about Grace." Archibald looked at Mumsfield. Blanche could see that he wanted to tell Mumsfield to leave the room again. But anyone looking at Mumsfield could see that would be of no use. Mumsfield sat down and reached for Blanche's hand across the table.

"There was always talk in the family," Archibald began. "Since she was a child…a cat mangled, the drowning of our cousin Lorisa in the pond out front, accidents to the servants' children." He looked like a man poring over photos of the past, trying to understand their relationship to one another. "But her parents and grandparents would hear nothing against her. Said she was high-strung, artistic. When she took up with Everett there was no one to stop her. Her parents were both dead. She was an only child. The fact that Everett was already married…" Archibald shrugged. "At any rate, they married, and…"

"What about Everett's first wife?" Mumsfield's grip on Blanche's hand became nearly crippling. She grimaced in pain.

"How do you know about these things?" Archibald looked as though he suspected her of having supernatural powers.

"Anyone could see she wasn't sane." Blanche stretched the truth just a bit. "And it's a small county," she added with a smile. "There ain't a lot of secrets."

"Why did she, Blanche? Why?" Mumsfield demanded to know.

"Because she's sick, Mumsfield, honey. In her mind. Very sick," she told him without hesitation. Mumsfield's grip loosened a bit.

Blanche was aware of Archibald's attentiveness to her response to Mumsfield. She felt the older man relax. She understood the relief he must have felt that Mumsfield's question was directed at her instead of himself. She also realized that the lack of hostility she saw on Archibald's face when she now looked fully at him was related to more than her answer to Mumsfield's question.

She and Archibald were going through a very speeded-up version of the de-jackassing process. While he might have defended blacks in court, it didn't mean he considered her his equal, any more than her employers did generally. Usually it took three to five cleaning sessions for a new employer of the racist jackass variety to stop speaking to her in loud, simple sentences. It took an additional fifteen to fifty substantive contacts before she was acknowledged as a bona fide member of the human race. Now here was Archibald already past the testing-your-intelligence phase, being mindful and grateful that she'd been smart enough and quick enough to help him out of a difficult situation with Mumsfield, one he clearly hadn't been prepared to handle. It gave Blanche an idea.

A burly, red-faced man knocked on the back door and asked for Archibald. Blanche went to fetch him and listened from behind the door while the man told Archibald that "the boys" had searched all the obvious places, like the quarry and the woods, but had found no trace of anything unusual—otherwise known as Everett, Blanche thought. Archibald told the man to bring the boys back in the morning and cautioned them to speak to no one.

When Archibald returned to the kitchen, Blanche was at the kitchen table with her head resting on her arms. The day had lasted too long and the numbness that had protected her from the shock of having her life threatened by a madwoman was wearing off.

"I believe there's just a bit more business to which we need attend, and then you can rest." Archibald spoke gently but firmly, as though he had some inkling that he wasn't going to have her attention much longer.

Despite her shock and fatigue, Blanche was quite attentive to Archibald's long, drawn-out speech about how grateful the family was for her good sense in contacting him instead of the authorities. As if he isn't one of them, she thought. He worked his way up to hoping she'd stay on as housekeeper and companion to Mumsfield at a salary that made her eyes sparkle. Blanche thanked him for the job offer and launched into the story of how she had come to be in the house.

Archibald looked shocked and then amused by Blanche's story. Apparently, the local justice system was not an object of his respect, either. He assured her that he could and would straighten out her difficulties first thing in the morning and once again offered her a job. Blanche rose from the table and walked to the window, where her Nate rock sat on its paper towel. She reached out and touched it, letting her fingers feel its cool, rough texture. She could hear Nate's sharp, dry voice reminding her of the number of chances for security a woman like her was likely to get in life.

"I got kids," she told Archibald. "They need health insurance and good schooling. And I want a ten-year contract. In writing. And a pension plan." Archibald merely nodded.

But still she couldn't agree. "Please, Blanche," Mumsfield said.

Blanche stared at Nate's rock and remembered how she'd gotten it. She thought how comfortable, how simple and safe her life could be working for Mumsfield—summer days of bird song and country peace, her kids digging in Nate's garden. But it was Nate's garden. He was supposed to be scooping up handfuls of loamy soil, filling his nose with its rich aroma, caking his fingernails with it while the sun crisped the back of his neck.

If Lucille showed up, she'd be paid off also, as would Everett—if he was alive. If he was dead, some convenient accident would be invented to explain his death, too. But what about Grace? What happened when she was let out, or the wily bitch escaped?

Blanche spun around and looked from one to the other of the two white men waiting for her to make up her mind to serve them, to preserve their secrets and their way of life by throwing herself like a big black blanket over what had happened here. But what about Nate? And even the sheriff? Wasn't somebody supposed to do something about their deaths beside cart the killer off to a cushy asylum and hire a housekeeper with hush money?

"Please, Blanche," Mumsfield repeated.

Blanche picked up her Nate rock and cradled it in both hands. "Let me think about it, Mumsfield, honey. Let me think about it." She tucked the rock in her pocket and went off to bed.

EPILOGUE

B lanche told everyone she needed a breather, so she was going to visit some friends in South Carolina. It wasn't true, of course. She was on her way to Boston to stay with Cousin Charlotte. She also hadn't told folks that she never expected to return to Farleigh, not even to get her kids. Ardell would bring Taifa and Malik to her when the time came. She hadn't told folks the whole truth because she thought it was best for her to be in a state of plans-and-whereabouts-unknown.

She'd be in Boston by the time the story broke in the *Atlanta Constitution*. The reporter had assured her that her name would not be mentioned, but Archibald would know. What would Archibald think when he realized he'd paid her all that money and she'd hardly gotten out the door before she was asking around for a reporter a person could halfway trust? Of course, she hadn't promised to keep her mouth shut, and she wasn't responsible for Archibald's assumptions. Aggravation pay, not hush money. She'd known all along that she could not keep quiet.

Her major goal had been to make sure that everyone around knew just how crazy Grace was, as a way of ensuring that she stayed locked up, for Nate's sake. It wasn't much, and it might not work, but it was all that she could think to do that would not land her in jail. She wondered whether Lucille would surface when it all came out. Archibald's boys had never been able to find Lucille, but Miz Minnie knew where she was. Miz Minnie had also found out, from the woman hired to look after Mumsfield, that Grace had tried to kill Everett with her favorite wrench. He'd managed to throw her out of the car but had been knocked out when the car swerved into a ravine. After Grace had left him for dead in the car, he'd managed to get the car out of the ravine and high-tail it to Atlanta in a panic. He'd since collected his clothes and whatever else he could get. Archibald had refused to give him any money, and Mumsfield had refused to see him or allow him to spend the night in the house. Everett had taken off for no one knew where. Blanche didn't mind that he'd gotten away. He was broke, prison enough for him, and he hadn't hurt anyone she cared about. Except Mumsfield, she added as an afterthought. She understood that his Down's syndrome made him as recognizably different from the people who ran and owned the world as she. It was this similarity that made him visible to her inner eye and eligible for her concern.

Their parting had been very sad. There was no way she could explain how the last six days had confirmed her constitutional distaste for being any white man's mammy, no matter what she thought of the man in question, or how many fancy titles and big salaries were put on the job. But while their parting was very sad, it was different from what she'd expected. She'd braced herself for his tears and pleading, his pitiful need for her. There had been tears in his eyes, but they'd stayed unshed. He'd neither pleaded nor looked pitiful.

"I understand, Blanche," he'd told her. "I understand." And for two seconds she'd thought that somehow he'd leaped across the gap between them and truly knew what it meant to be a black woman trying to control her own life and stand firm against having her brain vanillaed. She knew that she would think of him often, wonder what had become of him, how he'd aged. But she hoped never to see him or anyone connected to his family again.

Outside the bus window, trees and fields and farmhouses rushed by, as though running away from the skyscrapers, subways, and nightclubs she was moving toward. She'd thought about flying up to Boston but decided to use every nickel of the money Archibald had given her for Malik and Taifa's education.

She leaned back in her seat. She felt battered, as though the last six days had been one long fist fight that she hadn't exactly lost, but in which she'd been knocked about so badly that the way she saw and thought about things had been forever altered, although she couldn't yet put her finger on exactly how. She did know that while once she would have looked forward to city life, she was now approaching Boston as yet another enemy territory. It seemed that enemy territory was all there was in this country for someone who looked like her. She had nowhere else to go—at least to make a living—except among those who disdained her to death.

She knew she would step lightly again, dance, joke, laugh. She would always be a woman who'd come too close to murder, who knew what it meant to actually fear for her life. But, of course, that wasn't all of it. She smiled again at the memory of Grace lying unconscious at her feet. She would also always be a woman who'd fought for her life and won. That woman, no matter how much she'd changed, was still capable of negotiating enemy territory—even without a reference from her most recent employer.

ACKNOWLEDGMENTS

Blanche has had more mamas and midwives than a small nation, and I thank each and every one of them, most especially Jeremiah Cotton for his unflagging support, Kate White for her tireless editing, Helen Crowell for explaining Mosaicism to me, as well as Maxine Alexander, Taifa Bartz, Babs Bigham, Donna Bivens, Dick Cluster, Shelley Evans, Roz Feldberg, Charlene Gilbert, Lucy Marx, Ann, Vanessa, and Bryan Neely, and Barbara Taylor for their careful reading and invaluable comments.

ABOUT THE AUTHOR

 Barbara Neely's short fiction has appeared in various anthologies, including *Breaking Ice, Things That Divide Us, Angels of Power, Speaking for Ourselves,* and *Test Tube Women.* She lives in Jamaica Plain, Massachussetts, where she is working on the next Blanche White mystery.